Istnofret

Anna Loffman

PublishAmerica
Baltimore

First printing

ISBN: 1-4137-1748-9
PUBLISHED BY
PUBLISHAMERICA, LLLP.
www.publishamerica.com
Baltimore

Printed in the United States of America

Dedicated to Istnofret

ISTNOFRET
HEART

SLOWLY MY LIFEBLOOD EBBED AWAY. My breaths became shorter and my limbs became weaker. I was to join the gods now, even though I was younger than thirty. It was my destiny to die then.

Setiptah had left me then, and I had no more will to live. All I ever did was look after our children. Seeing Setiptah's eyes in each of theirs was too much to bear. This was no suicide. It was my day.

The pale face of Mos-Iye-Et fell back. I was dead at last, alone in my room. The ladies-in-waiting were to scream, shiver and then realise their duty. My children had to be moved—to live in the one place in Egypt where they shouldn't. To live in the noisy, eventful, evil place. The place where no child should live—the court of Thebes.

Unas, Bintat and Istnofret had never been moved before, and they were to make the same move their father did—from

Giza to Thebes. The ladies-in-waiting considered this to be their last duty, for they had homes in Giza.

As the palace came into view, the ladies-in-waiting shivered. Though the children really had to live here, each servant felt the sting of guilt that they had not adopted the poor souls themselves. The camels backed off a few paces and were reprimanded with lashes of the whip. Each one of those servants there was to regret their not adopting the children in time—they'd most likely hear nothing of the children from now, their living and their dying was all in the court's hands.

"Mmmschs…waste of time…shiachs… I accept grudgingly. And I never want to see you irritating servants again! Urgh. Here's a quarter of a deben of silver. Sort out the burial with that. Now go away, I have work to do."

Setiptah was sitting on the floor in a room covered with scrolls. The children sat there with him, confused and tired. They gazed at the women who wrinkled their foreheads in total pity. No help was offered to the young ones. They were to stay with their father.

The rich scribe clapped his hands. At this signal the servants left and a guard entered. "Take my children to the other end of the palace," he began, "and find them a lady-in-waiting there. Here's a whole deben of copper…." The guard's eyes lit up as Setiptah waved his hand over a huge chest. "Never seen that much money before?" he chuckled. "For it I want to hire that servant. If I ever catch sight of those little leeches again, I'm holding you personally responsible. Come here…" called Setiptah, with a hint of distaste in his voice. "You never dare tell that damn lady who sent you. You never dare tell those locusts who their father is. I'm not standing for begging letters. This money is for the frogs until they can look after themselves, you understand? Now get out of my sight, I can't stand the smell."

The guard was not surprised. Unas was the useful one; the

girls he did not want.

With great difficulty he hauled the massive wooden chest onto his shoulders and ordered the little ones over to him. The little ones, as they knew no better, tripped over in the direction of the voice which was calling them. Setiptah ignored them. Once again, he was deep in his scrolls. To all intents and purposes these small children were now helpless orphans.

When the young man was halfway down a beautiful corridor inscribed with hieroglyphics and decorated with paintings, he sat down and ordered the children to do so too. He divided the copper into sixths by the light of a small oil lamp. In Egyptian terms, he gave himself one-sixth and one-sixth of the copper. Towards Unas he pushed one-sixth, one-sixth and one-sixth of the money, and to the girls one-sixth. He stored the money in different compartments of the chest. Looking as normal as any guard could, he hauled the chest up once more and continued on his journey.

At the end of the court, where red coloured walls were exchanged for plastered ones almost luminous white, a young lady sat down on a stone slab near a sphinx. Her hair was bark-coloured and dirty looking but her eyes were the waves which lapped the shore, full of love and hope. She wasn't more than fifteen at the time, but she was strengthened and matured past her years by the hardship and life lessons of living in court. She was wearing a long white gown which was pleated at the back. The linen was somewhere between rough and fine, and she did not venture to hide it with jewellery or bring out the white of it with makeup. One short look at her was all the guard needed to see that she was poor and weak.

"I must ask something of you. I was walking in the palace with my son here, and I found these two orphan girls. My master refused to look after them. Here are my savings, I want you to have them if only you will look after the girls," he asked.

"What are their names?" she asked in reply.

"Written on their hair clips. I can't read, so I can't tell you. I take it you accept?"

"I do. But if I need more money, who shall I ask for?" The guard sighed.

"Butokhi," and then went on his way.

Without another word the girl took Bintat and Istnofret into her house.

Butokhi took Unas along the corridors further, happier now because the chest was lighter. A scribe with grey hair and a limp stumbled past them. "Wait, scribe!" called the guard. The old man turned. "If you read to me the name on this boy's tunic, I'll give you a copper coin."

Pleased with the offer, the scribe bent down slowly to look at Unas' tunic.

"Here it says 'Unas.'" Butokhi smiled, and gave the copper to the old scribe.

Unas and Butokhi walked briskly to the courtyard. Butokhi knew where to go to find the soldiers.

Finally they came upon the courtyard, with the sacred pool in the middle and greenery around it like a man-made oasis. "Here, Unas. You're four, aren't you?" asked Butokhi. Unas replied with a stiff, uncomfortable nod. "You are my son, Unas. My only son, Unas."

Butokhi was to show a generous side of himself to Unas. Unas was officially his son, and to be trained by a trusted soldier paid for by Butokhi. Unas was to live with Butokhi as his adopted son.

"Come here, my little daughters. Don't be afraid, harm will not befall you."

The tiny girls crawled towards Tionia. She carried them to a bed made of rough linen and straw, and laid them down to sleep. She felt sorry for the beautiful toddlers. Tionia lived with her mother as her mother was a widow. The toddlers would receive all of the love which she could give them and all the money that she may be able to afford.

The girls didn't know about Unas because Bintat was two and a half and Istnofret was one and a half. The adopted grandmother, Kiatoa, inspected the sleeping ones carefully. There was no doubt about it; they had once been rich.

Bintat slept quietly, her brown hair hanging by her ribs. The gods had blessed her with beautiful soft blue eyes.

Istnofret seemed disturbed by something; she did not lie still. Her blonde hair lay in curls down to her shoulders. The youngest one had deep brown eyes. You could catch a glimpse of the gorgeous chestnut colour when she opened her eyes in her sleep.

A year later, life seemed to be going well. Although the living standard was poor for the girls, they were loved wholeheartedly and unconditionally.

Tionia returned from a job in the fields in the evening to see little Istnofret playing outside. When she walked into the house, she saw the face of a pale little girl she thought she's never seen before. As she drew nearer, she recognised the face of her beloved Bintat.

White and trembling, Bintat fell on the floor as her legs lost strength. Tionia screamed and ran to her side. Her bloodshot eyes fell back in her head. The peasant girl felt for the temperature of the little one, and it was soaring. Tears appeared at Bintat's eyes. As she entered her death throes, her foster mother bent over by her to cradle her head. As Tionia could see the life was almost gone, she bent down to hear the child's last words.

"Mummy!" cried Bintat. "Mummy!" The tiny body went limp in Tionia's arms. Bintat had died aged three and a half.

Istnofret was called inside and she cried when she saw the body of her companion. Bintat would be buried out in the desert, with heavenly oases nearby to give a lullaby to her soul.

Kiatoa had never lost her strong belief in religion. What this belief was, however, was to be something for Istnofret to discover at a later date.

"Istnofret," she addressed the one who did not understand her words, "Bintat's unfinished life is in you. You own Bintat's spirit, Istnofret. You are two women, not one."

Istnofret's earliest memory was that of looking upon the face of her still beautiful but still sister, so different in appearance but so alike in heart. Bintat was laid on her side in the grave as if she was sleeping. The local scribe wrote upon the walls;

> 'Here lies the remainder of Bintat,
> One whom Ptah had called to live,
> Who now lives everlasting in Osiris,
> She who remembers not her life as We,
> She whom the gods controlled,
> She, the immortal soul,
> She rests here for eternity, Bintat.'

A little food and water was laid with her, so they may multiply and let her be well fed in the afterlife. Her hair clip and wood-bead necklace were decorating her so they may multiply and make her rich in the afterlife.

Istnofret watched all of the comings and goings without interest. As time went by, the little one learnt to speak, to understand, to run, to paint, to use mathematics—but in each step forward in her life was Bintat's discontented Kha.

Istnofret grew and became more intelligent, in a way denied to Bintat. Bintat was never intended to go through the trials of life—of work, of responsibility—she had none. Istnofret had to endure these and everything she achieved made Bintat's Kha happier.

The years passed and life without the blue-eyed girl became more normal. Though Tionia and Kiatoa tried as hard as they could, Istnofret lived the life of a peasant girl. Each morning she would fetch water from the wells and run errands for rich politicians or scribes. She took to wood-chopping or making the court's papyrus during the day. At nighttime she'd sneak out of bed like a criminal in the dark and learn from observing the palace painters binding words and pictures to create feelings. The girl worked hard, but secretly she was empty. Secretly she needed something to change.

Not knowing her purpose in life, Istnofret approached the wisest person she knew—Kiatoa—to tell her the answer. Kiatoa had looked right through her, which she had never done before.

"My daughter," began the lady, "each has a destiny. My destiny was to bring up three daughters, who will I pray be finally reunited by the Son of God at the end of time. You may have a humble life ahead, girl, but you have the fire of Bintat in your veins. Your heart is vast, my dear, your loyalty is strong. Your destiny will become clear, my dear, do not be impatient." Kiatoa lived a fine life and died with loved ones around her a year later. Her last words to Istnofret the eleven-year-old were; "Love, my love."

The girl lay in her uncomfortable straw bed, tossing and turning with heat pondering her grandmother's words. Her conclusion was to listen to Kiatoa's words, that her destiny would become clear. However she did not know who the Son of God was, and such crazy talk frightened her. This too she was to discover.

Istnofret had guessed correctly.

One night, Istnofret waited for the water clock to stop. This was not just any night; her fourteenth birthday was to be the day after. Extra food and boiled sweets flavoured with honey awaited her. Tionia was to invite some neighbours to sing and dance around a campfire. These were modest occasions but everyone enjoyed them very much.

The trickling sound stopped, and she set the water clock up to work again. When she sat up, she saw print marks on her body where the straw had left its imprint on her delicate skin. Looking in Tionia's broken mirror, she gasped. Those blonde curls which she had owned all her life were gone. Her hair was much longer now, and it was as straight as the country's borders. Istnofret was a young lady. She smiled at herself, and got dressed in a small white gown of the type which Tionia wore. Not bothering with cherry-juice on her lips or her hair clip, she slipped out of the modest dwelling without a sound.

Barefoot on the tiled floor she shivered a little but knowing her route through the court expertly she cleared the distance with silent speed. The pillars and walls seemed to be caving in on her but she showed no fear. Tonight was yet another night when she was to observe the painters.

When the young girl hurried to where she always saw the painters, she noticed they'd moved on to another wall nearby. They were drawing out the grid squares which she'd seen them draw so many times before. Hiding behind a particularly elaborate pillar, she gazed at the fire of their lamps. The wall was lit from the bottom, so the shadows of the young painters fell upon the ceiling. Istnofret stood flat to the pillar as a cat would, careful to hide the tassels of her dress from another's sight.

A young man walked through a hole in the wall which must have been a doorless front door. His jet-black hair was uneven. It was clear to see that he was trying to outgrow his sidelock of youth which hung unattractively to his shoulders. This man walked with stunning dignity. He seemed indifferent to the fact that he was working at this unholy hour. Something about this man made him different from the painters. It was not his clothes, nor the way he looked, but possibly his pride which someone could even sense from a distance of twenty metres.

His eyes were grey and his nose was large but not unsightly. Anyone could judge that he was no weakling quite easily. His kilt hung from his hips with a yellow band around the top. It was traditionally decorated, with a vertical pleat in the front to decorate it. The man was tall, with long, muscular legs and sandaled feet.

Istnofret shivered all over and her heart leapt into her mouth. She had a strange feeling that she was falling suddenly and then being caught. Gazing at the man, she almost forgot her hiding place. The girl turned, back to the pillar. Her heart thudded. Her knees felt weak so she slid to the floor. She smiled nervously, and looked to the heavens from where this man had obviously come. Much to her surprise, the man seemed to be walking straight at her.

The young man had checked the work of the painters. His job was done. Walking down the pillared hall, he caught sight of a shuffle of movement behind a pillar. He smiled, and walked back to his ebony engraved bed.

Istnofret awoke the next morning to hear Tionia playing a reed instrument. As she opened her eyes, Tionia gave a huge grin.

"I met you this day thirteen years ago!" she laughed, giving the pale girl a boiled sweet.

"Thank you, Tionia. But Mother—I have to go to get the water. I'll come back soon!"

"That's very kind of you. I'll have dates, bread and honey waiting for you when you return."

Istnofret tried to look delighted that it was her birthday when in actual fact she couldn't care less.

As she got out of the plastered house, she ran to the nearest scribe's office. When she entered, the sun was pouring through the windows like water.

"What do you want?" he demanded, as he looked up from his time-consuming papyri. Istnofret spoke slowly, her mind racing faster than her mouth.

"In order to find a painter my father wishes to hire, I must know who was overseeing the palace painters at midnight last night."

"All right then, give me a description, girl."

"He has grey eyes and black hair. He's outgrowing his sidelock of youth…?" She looked up. The scribe's face glowed with inspiration. He ran out to another room in the office. Istnofret sat impatiently, drumming her fingers against her arm.

The tired scribe returned to her.

"My lady," he began sarcastically, "you will need to speak to Prince Ramesses. I do believe he'll be drinking cheap beer in the Hall of Columns tonight with his brother, Prince Shanaar. Good luck with your, ahem…" he laughed, "painter."

Istnofret didn't care that the scribe had seen right through her. She was shocked that it was a prince, and yet she saw that this made perfect sense. Uttering the promise of a favour, the stunned peasant-girl made her way to the well. Gathering a large amount of water in buckets, she returned to Tionia's house. Greeted by a genuine smile, Istnofret thought she'd tell her mother the truth.

"I'm in love, Tionia!" she managed to squeak. Tionia extended her smile. "Oh, we all think we are at your age. Now come; enjoy your breakfast."

Tionia's casual manner relieved Istnofret. Istnofret did indeed manage to enjoy her day. But that night, she crept out of bed and tiptoed to the Hall of Columns.

The hall stood empty looking. The only furniture was a small altar at the front. Istnofret thought, sneezing at the breath of pollen in the air.

The princes walked through the door. The hall stood empty looking once more.

Istnofret awoke in the early hours of the morning. When she tried to sit up, she hurt her head loudly against the top of the table. A bronze statue of Ma'at came crashing down.

"Be *careful*, brother," moaned Ramesses in his sleep, as Istnofret crept out from under the decorative cloth, taking one last look at Ramesses and sneaking back to Tionia's house.

Surely the prince should be in love with her, because she loved him. This was her only comforting thought. Without motivation she soon became depressed. Still, whenever she could bring herself to she'd crawl into the palace at night to fall asleep to the sound of Ramesses' breathing. When she'd wake, she'd crawl back to Tionia's house.

One night, the tables turned. The girl was sixteen. This was against her will. Quickly, she crept into the palace once more. She had not lost the talent to hide by any means. But tonight was different. The girl hid behind a pillar, as usual.

She listened to the soft beat of the prince's breath. But for the first time ever, someone started reading the hieroglyphics on her pillar! Terrified, the petite teenager huddled herself into a ball even smaller. The man moved round the pillar, and almost shoved his flaming torch into Istnofret's face.

Istnofret calmed herself without making a sound, so as not to wake her beloved. Thinking of the prince, she dropped her guard as the man seized her wrists.

"Guards!" he yelled. "Guards!" There Istnofret decided on a policy. This was silence. She took as many deep breaths as she could before the prince's bodyguards appeared.

"Take this one to him," one ordered.

"What's your name?" asked the other, gruffly. Istnofret said nothing. The girl was slapped and kicked several times but her mouth remained firmly motionless.

Ramesses, alarmed by the sounds of the slaps and kicks upon Istnofret, stepped outside his room. The guards stopped attacking her the moment they saw him.

"Why are you here?" asked Ramesses in an authoritative tone. The look in her eyes spoke volumes. Her tongue spoke nothing. Commanding his bodyguards to leave him, he beckoned Istnofret inside his beautiful bedroom.

Istnofret felt like fainting, overwhelmed by the events and exhausted by the day before. But here she was, alone with Prince Ramesses in a place where his rugged smell filled even the tiniest alcove. Ramesses could now make her talk.

"Why are you here, girl?" he asked again. Istnofret, petrified, told him the honest and pathetic truth.

"To check that you're still...breathing?" she blurted out. The prince giggled at the sheer sight of the person. But this giggle at her choice of words he could not stifle. "Oh yes...?" he teased.

She looked him in the eyes as sincere as I am now and said; "I'm in love with you, Prince Ramesses, and though this involves you please don't think more of it as I know the love can never be returned."

The prince seemed to take in everything she said, and what's worse, seemed to agree—until the next time she looked at him he kissed her with such speed she almost had a heart attack.

"Now go. Sleep well. Maybe I will see more of you..."

"Istnofret." Istnofret finished his sentence. The prince then turned his back on Istnofret, climbing into his bed. The girl crept out of his room speedily.

If only Istnofret knew that Ramesses was also lying awake, thinking of her. The first half of the hours he now owned were dedicated to working out 'how do I tell Mother and Father?' but the second half was devoted to 'why should I tell Mother and Father?' What did he need their authority for? As the younger prince, his life's task was to enjoy himself. But would the pursuit of this task allow the prince to be seen with the peasant? Sure, he wasn't going to be Pharaoh, but Tuya would proclaim that he was lowering the Ramesside standard.

Something attracted the prince to this determined blonde.

Perhaps it was that he could see the emotion she felt for him in her eyes. He wanted to find out more about her; how long had she been in love with him? *Destiny*, thought Ramesses. *You can't argue with destiny.*

Istnofret lay in her straw bed confused. *Why did he kiss her? Was he in love with her like she hoped? Who was the man who caught her?* Of him, she remembered only his red hair. How would she explain her prominent bruises to Tionia?

Once again she picked up the broken mirror. She saw the face the prince thought pretty, with bruises high on the cheeks, wounds on the forehead and a split lip. But when she opened her chestnut eyes, her face became beautiful. Her hair was a mess from the struggle to escape the merciless punishment dealt out by the guards. Istnofret remained timid, with little to nothing hiding her bones. She knew that she must be careful of Ramesses. If he instructed it to, his almighty arm could crush her to the ground in seconds. But the giant was kind. She could see this in his face.

Istnofret fell into a troubled sleep, and awoke to hear Tionia shouting; "Whatever has happened to you, dear?" Istnofret looked at herself in the daylight. Her body was black, blue and purple with bruises.

"Mother!" she cried. "It wasn't a dream!" Tionia, curious at Istnofret's joy at seeing her blackened body, begged her to explain. Istnofret told Tionia everything.

"You've a gift, dear!" she complimented her. "Shame Shanaar didn't oversee the painters that night!" In fits of divine laughter, mother and daughter delighted together, laughing in the face of destiny's kind twist.

When the ladies calmed down, Tionia told Istnofret that she'd found a scroll in the doorway of the house. Istnofret unrolled it. She noted how elaborate it was. At the bottom was the seal of Seti I, with his cartouche in perfect red paint. Istnofret needed to find out what it said.

Tionia moaned; "It costs so much money to write, seal, post and read a scroll I've no idea why people do it. Why won't the Prince come and see you instead?"

"How much money have we got in the house..." asked Istnofret, ignoring Tionia, "in debens?"

"Can't say in debens," answered Tionia, "more like half a coin's worth of copper." Istnofret's face collapsed in despair.

Tionia's memory spoke. "Istnofret!" she exclaimed. "The man who said he'd found you promised money if we ever needed it. He said his name was... Butokhi, that's right, Butokhi. He has a son."

The women began their journey to the courtyard in high spirits but found it impossible to find one guard with one son. Giving up, Tionia set up a tent. Istnofret asked that she might be allowed to be alone with her thoughts.

It was then that Istnofret wandered outside the court for the second time in her life. She saw the life-giving Nile, the borderless desert and the court's high walls which no longer confined her. Free and amongst nature, she slept underneath the foliage of a young tree. How she fell asleep she'd never know. Was it the exhaustion of the night before? But when it was midday, and the sun was beating upon her bare shoulders, little did she care. She slept silently and happily, and for a long time.

"Istnofret!" came a voice. "Istnofret, wake up! It's me! You've gone red! Istnofret!" Istnofret opened her eyes briefly but did not register her surroundings. Instead, she fainted.

The man who found her carried her to a sheltered spot underneath a massive, drooping acacia tree. She was given water repeatedly. The girl finally awoke for good, staring into the eyes of Prince Ramesses.

"Heatstroke!" he exclaimed.

"Ramesses!" she managed to utter. "Ramesses!"

Istnofret felt terribly sick with the evil fever which took Bintat away from her.

As Prince Ramesses took a cup of water to her lips, she used her last amount of strength to kiss his fingertips. Ramesses looked upon Istnofret's face, white and weak, while she slept. The prince didn't leave her side until she woke again. She was as hot as the desert sand. He saw the girl trying to speak, and told her not to. She saw the worry in his eyes. He saw the pain in hers. Prince Ramesses cared for her, but would not get any outside help. Ramesses' feelings for the girl were strictly private. So he stayed by her bedside, morning and night, until finally she recovered from this.

Awake in the shade she noticed she was no longer ill, but Ramesses had gone to fetch water for her. Istnofret was amazed how quickly she'd found that Ramesses cared for her. She couldn't get over it. Still, Ramesses would not say he loved her. Istnofret couldn't understand this.

Tionia was probably looking for Istnofret's body. Luckily for both of them, there was still some life in it.

Ramesses returned to see the girl in perfect health. The smile she gave him was his reward for tireless nursing. Although a confusion to all but themselves, what followed seemed perfectly natural for the prince and the peasant by the banks of the Nile.

Prince Ramesses fell asleep. Istnofret looked at him carefully. He was twenty. He looked stronger than he had before. Her heart skipping a beat, Istnofret kissed the prince good night and crept away from the acacia. She did this for Ramesses, because if they were to wake with a roof over their heads they were married. Istnofret would force nothing on Ramesses.

In the morning, she knew not what hour, she returned to Tionia. Tionia was exhausted but delighted to listen to her daughter's exploits. She was the only person other than the two to know. The prince was counting on her to keep her mouth shut. He preferred not to think of what might happen if she didn't.

Tionia was not harsh towards Istnofret for disappearing without trace or communication. Istnofret thought that she was surprisingly calm in the circumstances. Together Istnofret and Tionia watched the sun rise. Such amazing happiness accompanied them.

Ramesses awoke with a start. He sat up, terrified, bolt alert. Prince Ramesses had forgotten the law of marriage! How could he keep Istnofret a secret if she was married to him? Dizzily, he looked around himself. First he noted that there were no witnesses to anything. Eventually he realised that Istnofret had gone. Hand on his heart Ramesses sighed, falling asleep the moment his head hit the grass.

Istnofret decided to do some investigating. She walked down to the palace in bright daylight. Sheltering behind a sacred bush, she looked from the garden into the palace hall. Istnofret certainly wasn't meant to be there. She wanted to be so she was.

Though the foliage partially hid her view, she saw with relative ease. The main hall was magnificent.

Istnofret saw her leader; her Pharaoh, with nothing on but a small grey kilt yelling orders at his poor servants. She giggled. She reckoned she could probably knock him senseless with a single punch if it wasn't for those serious-looking brutish guards surrounding him. Seti I stood before her yet she felt no respect. Actually, what seemed amusing to her was the Seth in him. When he was a young man, he must have been a passionate, furious force to be reckoned with. Now he was crazy, little and old, and he yelled things at men twice his size. They treated him as if he was ten feet tall and armed. To think that Ramesses would once be like him made her laugh even more.

Grumpy Seti almost totally cleared the scene until his wife appeared. Tuya commanded respect and in her presence you could feel her wisdom. The queen's age-weary face demanded awe from the population. Tuya showed such a love for her husband you could see it shining in her eyes.

Istnofret noticed how unusual Tuya looked. She had thick brown hair and small brown eyes. Serious and thoughtful, she was set apart from Istnofret's generation—that which she was so connected to.

Another prince came to talk to the queen. Istnofret didn't know that he was Amon-Her-Khasimweh but she could tell that he was level-headed and careful. As a matter of fact, he attracted more attention from the female population than any other prince and took no apparent notice. His thin black hair was shoulder length. He had blue eyes like Prince Ramesses.

Istnofret smiled to herself. She walked silently back from the palace. Tionia laughed like never before at Istnofret not being smitten with Amon-Her-Khepertikhokha like everyone else. She had a rather different view of the aged Pharaoh, but she had seen him in his more youthful days.

Istnofret asked Tionia about Ramesses I.

"If only Kiatoa were here, my dear!" she replied. But everyone knew that Ramesses I had been old when he came to the throne. He only became Pharaoh because of Seti and Shanaar. When Dynasty 18 was on its last legs, a military man was chosen to rule as it was the dynasty before. Istnofret asked Tionia about times before Ramesses I. Tionia looked to the heavens.

"Listen, girl!" she hissed. "I'm breaking the law. There was once a time when everyone was free and the Sun God controlled all. Egypt was a society based on peace and religious tolerance, not to mention tolerance of sexuality and equal opportunities. A wonderful king reigned. His name was Akhenaten Neferkheperure, and he had many children…."

"Atenist!" growled Istnofret, under her breath.

"Yes, Atenist. So the Pharaohs hated the Sun God and the Son of God from then forwards. What a threat to the powerful priests of Amun the Aten was! Still, do we not allow I Am within the boundaries of our country?" challenged Tionia.

"We do not allow the Hebrews to sacrifice cats. We will never, ever allow Akhenaten to destroy our faith again!" Tionia sighed.

"He merely showed us the light, that no man may come to God but through him! Open your eyes."

"My eyes are wide open and do you know what I see?" she asked. "I see a man who so craved power he would have the arrogance to suggest that only he could be in touch with a created god who every Egyptian noble must worship! I see a man who had such weakness he would have others work with foreign policy without a Pharaoh! I see a man who exiled his wife, went mad and had a relationship with his own son!" Istnofret saw a papyrus by the door.

"Seti spends Egyptian lives trying to destroy the misled race that is the Atenists. One here… Don't blame me if I never return!"

Tionia cried like never before. Tears dropped to her knees. The wails of a devastated mother showed the world the cruelty of religion.

Istnofret shook with anger. How dare she forget the true gods? At the same time she felt forbidden to empty her heart to her lover. What little care she had left for Tionia wouldn't let the royal family treat her like they usually treated Atenists. Instead she just made her way to the shade of the acacia.

There Prince Ramesses stood in all his splendour, shoulders set back and shining black hair. Gold shined upon him. He gazed at her with a sleepy look in his eyes. To Istnofret he looked irresistible, but he mustn't have been so.

"Why have you brought me here?" the girl demanded. Ramesses said nothing, but continued to gaze dreamily at Istnofret. The confused little peasant redirected her anger to Prince Ramesses. "I'll go then, shall I?" she yelled. As she turned her back on Ramesses, she felt his soft fingers on the back of her bare arm. He uttered the words which came into his throat.

"Marry me!" The girl's jaw dropped. It was clear he meant what he had said. Unable to remain furious for long, the normally passive teenager showered Prince Ramesses with passion as he had decided it was what he needed.

Istnofret awoke to feel the prince's nose nudging hers. She ran her fingers through his hair. The sun rose, and so it became that Prince Ramesses and Istnofret were married. The girl forgot the night before almost completely and made for Tionia's house after kissing Ramesses goodbye.

The stray girl was welcomed back like the prodigal son and she learnt to accept the differences between herself and her mother. As an Amunist by nature this took some time, but she was to learn of religious tolerance—which Akhenaten had taught.

In that plaster-white doorway of Tionia's house, Istnofret spotted another piece of papyrus. It seemed there was no satisfying the young man—but she was wrong. As she eyed the piece of plain papyrus, she failed to notice the tear marks on the surface. Unknowingly, she went down to the Nile. She expected her love. She found nothing. Contented, Istnofret fell into a deep sleep in the shade of the acacia where Ramesses had looked after her.

When Istnofret awoke, it was nighttime and someone had lit a fire nearby. It was Ramesses!

"Our prince!" mumbled Istnofret.

"Yes, Istnofret. It's me I think…" stuttered the noble. He had little childish sarcasm which he usually kept. "Father is dying, Istnofret. We must go to him to receive his blessing before he goes on." The peasant was impressed. This was thoughtful of Ramesses.

The couple were to visit Pharaoh the following morning. Istnofret had Ramesses' idea explained to her.

"Father is dying of earth-age. All of my family will be with him tomorrow. He says that he has some honours to give and some last words for us all. He needs witnesses."

Istnofret knew, however, that she was witnessing the inevitable. In the next Pharaoh's favour, Prince Ramesses would enjoy a luxurious lifestyle and the ability to keep Istnofret at home.

Istnofret awoke staring into Ramesses' beautiful eyes. They were red from crying. The girl was shaken to realise how much the father and son loved each other.

The peasant dressed in the most respectable dress she owned. She set about crushing leaves and cherries to use as makeup. The Pharaoh must see her looking her best, though Ramesses preferred her looking bright red, bruised all over…

Ramesses looked stunning as usual but they went in disguise. The prince may not be seen with the peasant. The sleepy palace guards ventured not to bother the suspicious-looking pair. They entered the palace quietly. A shawl hid Istnofret's face and odd blonde hair.

The charming prince lead her to Seti's bedroom. All of the times that she had crept into the palace she had gone to Ramesses'.

The door was beautifully engraved but a cloak of mourning hung over it. The son pushed it open.

There was Tuya in all her grace. Seti lay in his bed, silent and thoughtful. Pharaoh's sons crowded around him. The most notable ones were Prince Amon-Her-Khepertikhokha and Prince Shanaar. One of them, who Istnofret was to find out was called Mnao, was very upset. Mnao was just fifteen.

The couple arrived late. They stood at the back of the crowd. Pharaoh was to give his dying speech.

"My family," he began, "the ones who have made my life so

sweet. I wish for you to witness my declaring of the man—" Tuya coughed, "or woman who is to be my successor. I believe him to be of almighty wisdom, unchallengeable dignity, traditional splendour, iron fist…." Prince Shanaar grinned. It was a privilege for Seti to have devoted most of his dying speech to him. "Strong bull, He who will Unite the Two Lands once again, my son…" Shanaar made himself ready to heartily thank his dear father.

"Ramesses!"

The whole room became silent. Shanaar could not believe his ears. He was still shocked when the sons parted to form a passageway through to Ramesses. All at once, Istnofret was seen. They both walked to the bed. Tuya was the only one still standing by Seti.

"I cannot accept, Father," stammered Ramesses. A cry went up. "For I am married to this young lady."

"Does not the law of the Two Lands state that no throne is stable without a Great Royal Wife?" quoted Seti. "Is it not forbidden for a Pharaoh to marry a peasant-girl?" retorted the prince. Shanaar almost laughed in his changeable state.

"Ramesses, I recognise a noble's face in this girl. She's not a peasant. Keep her as a secondary wife, son—till you can prove my thought." The whole family was overwhelmed by such drama. Pharaoh turned to Istnofret and spoke with great dignity. "You knew not your parents. I think I have known one. I recognise the light in your eyes, girl—a light I'll never forget. I believe one of your parents still lives."

Unable to reply, everyone just stared. It was clear that Pharaoh was sober. He was not mentally ill. Prince Shanaar had still not recovered from the shock of not being chosen. He had been brought up and trained solely to become Pharaoh! Ramesses bowed his head, and Seti placed his hands upon it. The kingdom was accepted.

Amon-Her-Khasimweh looked on with great happiness. He knew that Seti had chosen the right one. A handshake and a grin between the two handsome brothers was the first congratulations which Ramesses received, Istnofret being too stunned to speak.

"Mother!" Ramesses called. "Meet Istnofret!" It was nervously that Istnofret took Tuya's hand. It was then that Istnofret discovered those age-weary veins, sticking from the skin as if permanently separate. Tuya said nothing, knowing it was better to do this than to speak her mind. It was hard enough for the queen to comprehend life without Seti. He was always her brave, strong warrior. He remained as handsome as ever but only in her eyes. She had never experienced such pain as to see him deteriorate and to be unable to see him. Tuya had always been a solid woman. She had cried only once when her only daughter, and last child, was stillborn. Anyone could see that there were years yet to come within Tuya. Tuya dazzled Istnofret, but it was clear to see that Istnofret was not in favour in the queen's eyes.

That was indeed a day full of surprise. Istnofret gained respect for Seti. She learnt to trust him. As Tionia was told the story, she leapt into the air with glee.

"Superb!" she stuttered. "Superb!"

It was a week until Istnofret's seventeenth birthday when she first became suspicious. Three weeks later it was proved by tests that she was pregnant. Not knowing how to tell the tearful prince, she opted not to but to beg to see Pharaoh instead. Eventually the guards let her in but only to stay for a short while. The door to Seti's bedroom opened. Istnofret ran to his side.

"My daughter…" Seti began, "I cannot see you but I know who you are. I recognise the sound of bare feet. Come closer—take my hands." Upset, Istnofret knelt and held Seti's hands.

"Pharaoh, I am pregnant," Istnofret announced, her deepest fear reflecting in her voice. Seti's weary face smiled.

"My very own grandson. Look after him well, Istnofret—and break the tradition. Don't name him after me. You name someone Seti only when they have Seth in themselves." Istnofret gulped.

"I will try to look after him well, but Pharaoh… I am afraid."

A sense of warning existed in Seti's voice. "You must have my grandson, daughter. Take care of him. You must look after him well. Does Ramesses know yet?" he asked. An ashamed reply came back to Istnofret.

"Tell him after I die. I think that I will not be able to remain here for much longer, Istnofret. But I sense a loyalty in you, my daughter, which makes you fit for my son," Seti assessed. Istnofret bowed her head and left the palace solemnly.

It was true that Istnofret flinched the very moment that Seti died. She told Tionia. Minutes later messengers were sent out to tell of Pharaoh's death.

Mother and daughter were not openly upset, but each shed a tear in private for the wise old king.

Istnofret did not disturb Ramesses. It looked as if he intended to cope with his grief alone. He wanted this to begin with, but nature was to change all that.

How frightened she was! Poor young Istnofret spent nights praying, crying, hoping and wondering. It seemed that if she didn't tell him soon he'd work it out for himself. Tionia was the only one to know. No reassuring could comfort the girl. She knew she'd be staring death in the face at birth.

Prince Ramesses thought nothing of Istnofret after Seti's death. He briefly forgot her existence. The twenty-one-year-old simply spent all of his time in the temples. He could not bear to speak. He said nothing for a week. He also fasted repeatedly. The heir was contemplating life. He therefore needed space and time. Seti was to be buried in a few months time and each day was a help for Ramesses.

The temple of Hathor was a true masterpiece; its balconies

and statues and flowers hanging everywhere. Here in the home of the goddess of love, Ramesses' memory was not jolted at all. He bowed his head in prayer.

The beautiful musician ran lightly across the cold floor, her feet bare as a sign of respect. A large, hooded cloak worn over a baggy black dress showed her extreme modesty. She didn't notice Ramesses.

The prince looked up, and he felt as though something had stuck his heart.

ISTNOFRET HANDS

IT WAS SOME MONTHS LATER when Istnofret decided she could bear Ramesses' peace no longer. The mourning period was nearly over, Ramesses' coronation was soon to take place and the declaration of Istnofret as secondary wife. The menacing bump in her stomach was growing. Soon rumours would begin to spread. The heir had to hear the truth from her, so she entered the palace shyly but with purpose.

"Who are you?" grunted the guards. Something compelled her to give herself a false title.

"King's Wife, King's Mother, Istnofret," Istnofret replied. The baffled guards let her continue on her way.

Istnofret hid once more where she had hidden before. She crouched down in the alcove behind the pillar near Ramesses' door. It was daylight, but she heard Ramesses' heavy breathing coming from the room. The sound of footsteps echoed through to Istnofret's ears. As the girl stepped up to the door, she hesitated. The smell of newly burned incense struck her. When she heard something from inside, she put her ear to the door.

"You made the right decision coming here, Nefertari," said Ramesses.

A sweet voice replied.

"What have you brought me here to say, Ramesses?" Silence followed.

"Well—not very much, really…" Ramesses replied awkwardly. Innocent Nefertari hadn't awoken to Ramesses' mind the way that Istnofret had.

"How does that make sense?" she continued.

The prince lost his patience. "Like this," he replied.

More silence followed. Soon, Istnofret heard fairly sharp gasps. Istnofret slunk down, hanging her head. Tears came to her eyes which she refused to let roll. It was what her husband wanted. She needed him to be happy. Istnofret wanted to be Nefertari—so innocent, given the right to be allowed to be seen in the palace with Ramesses.

The blonde girl heard Ramesses sigh like she'd heard him before. As if she wasn't in control of anything, Ramesses' breathing sent her to sleep again.

Something slimy was running through her hair. Trying to stay calm, she refused to scream and put a finger to it. *It was a snake! It was a massive snake!* Her eyes grew wide and she started panting like never before.

"Ha ha! Got you there! You should've seen your face, erm—'miss'!" laughed Amon-Her-Khasimweh. When he lifted the harmless snake from her hair, he set it free. He noticed her bump.

"You're pretty gorgeous for a little peasant, aren't you?" Istnofret looked up at the prince.

She said clearly and with confidence; "I am married to your brother!" Quick realisation followed.

"You mean you came to tell him…"

"Yes, and found him…"

"Precisely. Come here, sister." Istnofret didn't understand Amon-Her-Khasimweh but he beckoned her near. The prince gave her a reassuring hug. "We'll go in there together, lady, and I'll stay by your side."

Thanks would have been too little for what the prince had done for Istnofret. She went limp in his arms. She let him pull her up and help her over to the door.

The strong, tanned knuckles of Amon-Her-Khasimweh rapped against the door. No reply came from inside.

The younger prince knew that Ramesses wouldn't be happy to be woken. He opened the door anyway.

The room was a mess. Clothes were everywhere. In the middle of the floor the two slept soundly. It was as if the two asleep were in paradise. Istnofret and Ramesses had never slept so close. The couple were white.

Amon-Her-Khasimweh yelled in Ramesses' ear. Ramesses awoke. He looked around himself. He saw the Perfect One, asleep and more beautiful than ever. He saw his brother and secondary wife. The bump he did not see.

"Ramesses!" exclaimed Istnofret. The word flew from her mouth like a dove. "I am carrying your child!" Ramesses stood up, naked as the day he was born, and put his hands upon Istnofret's swollen stomach. The baby kicked. Ramesses smiled.

Nefertari opened her eyes. They were a beautiful deep sea blue. When she saw Ramesses and Istnofret, she smiled with her fleshy red lips. He had a child on the way!

It was then that the paths of the two ladies' eyes met. There was no hatred, just a deep understanding. Istnofret's jealousy had vanished forever. There was no competition between them; Nefertari was beauty personified. Istnofret didn't waste her time thinking as we think. From the start the women respected each other for what they were to Ramesses.

Grins broke out on the faces of all present. There could have been sweat, blood and tears but there were none.

Istnofret told all to Tionia. The mother still couldn't believe she didn't find Amon-Her-Khasimweh attractive.

Unfortunately, as it was to turn out, the girl told the truth.

Ramesses and Nefertari sat by the Pool of Atum, created at the beginning of time to last through eternity. The conversation was faint, worthless. Nefertari's eyed pierced Ramesses through. He remained in awe of her there.

"You don't need to persuade me anymore, Ramesses." She looked at him. Ramesses stood honest in a world of confusion. He was terrified of her reaction.

"I… I think Nefertari, I'm in love with you," he stammered. Nefertari fell into Ramesses' arms. He breathed a sigh of relief.

The respected ones, the priestesses of Hathor, were fussing around Istnofret. Not only did they prescribe medicines and potions to physically help her and the baby but also ones to ward off evil spirits. Istnofret knew she wouldn't be looked at twice during the coronation. The ladies of the temple had other ideas.

Istnofret dreamt of her husband. When she took notice, she heard the priestesses having a raging row over her neckline.

Istnofret decided to take a walk in the gardens to calm her spirits and to meditate.

The gorgeous foliage of the stunning trees and plants stretched out before her like the night sky. The flowers were twinkling stars—forever there and forever in numbers. Stunning waterways glistened in the sun, partially shaded by the trees carrying the softest, sweetest fruit you could imagine. The vast area of grass built a sense of peace about the place. The peace would exist for all eternity.

Nefertari came here. Istnofret did not know this. It was a noble's secret garden. Istnofret had stumbled upon it by chance.

Under a great palm Istnofret sat to meditate. She was almost unaware of the two men walking towards her.

"So you say Seti granted me a house before he died, Toto?" the old man asked.

"Yes, in return for your loyal service to his favourite scribe. Nice work, Butokhi."

The name echoed inside Istnofret. She drew to the surface her memory of Tionia's words.

"Butokhi!" she called. "I am Istnofret!"

The retired guard stared. He was never told the names of Bintat and Istnofret. He had no idea who she was. As the peasant obviously wanted to speak with him, he asked Toto to wait a while. Butokhi walked carefully to Istnofret.

"I am an orphan-girl you gave to Tionia to look after nearly sixteen years ago. You have a son, don't you? You gave my mother a sixth of a deben of copper to look after myself and my sister Bintat…?"

Butokhi thought hard. It took him some time. He managed to recall this. Just before he adopted Unas he did indeed give a peasant his sisters, and a sixth of a deben.

"Yes," he said at last, "I know who you are."

Unas leapt at his father's call. He ran two hundred metres in a flash. Despite not knowing who this lady was, he bowed low before her out of politeness. The story was once more related to Unas.

"We shall go to see Setiptah after the birth of Pharaoh's son," Unas suggested. He tapped his sister's stomach.

Istnofret nodded. Already she was proud of her long-lost brother. She went back to Tionia happy. As always, she told her mother everything honestly. Tionia listened with a good ear.

It was this time when Ramesses and Nefertari spent all their days together. The two actually married on the morning of the coronation. Istnofret was very pleased for Ramesses. He was now coping with Seti's death with a strong and positive mind.

All the rituals were celebrated. All Thebes got drunk. The feasting in the evening was truly magnificent. The wine was stupendous. At the end of the meal, Istnofret sat under the bough of a great tree with Prince Amon-Her-Khasimweh. Ramesses had different ideas and ran through the palace with Nefertari.

It shouldn't have been so according to the ancient doctors—because she took all that was prescribed—but Istnofret went into labour right there, seven months pregnant.

She had never known such pain or exhaustion. For hours it was touch and go whether or not she would live through it. Amon-Her-Khasimweh was there with her, and refused to desert her.

The prince cut the umbilical cord and washed the baby in the Nile. He uttered the words she was longing to hear;

"It's healthy, Istnofret—they were right—it's a boy!" She grinned in her awful state and murmured a thanks before falling into a deep, undisturbed sleep.

"I took the baby to the palace nurses," Amon-Her-Khasimweh began, "and I left your wife in the charge of the ladies-in-waiting. Congratulations, Pharaoh!" The brothers could not keep the smiles from their faces.

"You delivered my firstborn son on the night of my coronation." Ramesses laughed. "May you forever be the King's Friend."

Amon-Her-Khasimweh stepped backwards. Even then to be given such a title for such a good turn seemed to trouble him. Upon seeing the willingness and sincerity in Pharaoh's eyes, Amon-Her-Khasimweh embraced Ramesses. He simply couldn't decline—though he almost felt he wanted to.

"Do we have a name?" inquired the prince.

"Khaemwaset, Khaemwaset."

~ ~ ~

The lady-in-waiting looked at Nefertari and Nefertari looked at the lady-in-waiting. The queen's beautiful face was worried underneath the makeup and jewellery.

"Congratulations..." joked the servant. Nefertari collapsed in tears. She was pregnant. Young and vulnerable, the queen didn't know where to turn. "Go to Istnofret," advised the servant, "and talk to her."

She was distraught. The black-haired lady went to see Istnofret. There she lay on the floor of her bedroom, saying nothing and disturbing no one. Her eyes did not move as the Princess of All Women entered.

"The boy's name is Khaemwaset, I hear," began Nefertari. As Istnofret glanced elegantly upwards, Nefertari lost her dignity and broke down in her presence. Her soothing words helped Nefertari to regain the gift of speech.

"The doctors said...they said any child of mine didn't have a chance. It would...give the risk of killing me..." she sniffed. Istnofret knew.

"See Ramesses, he'll let you have an abortion," Istnofret suggested. The tearful lady shook her head. "They said I'm as weak as a kitten. They said...they said any potion strong enough to kill an unborn baby was strong enough to kill me. Oh, Istnofret, I stare death in the face!"

"You are my sister. I am beside you always. Ramesses is yours, therefore I am too."

The wise words were not enough for Nefertari. She left in tears as she had come.

Istnofret's health improved and soon she could sit and later stand. Tionia helped her all through. Her stomach was a little stretched, but that was only to be expected.

Two weeks after the birth, King's Friend Prince Amon-Her-Khasimweh visited her with tiny Khaemwaset in his arms. The boy was the size of a small forearm. His blonde wisps of hair were complimented by highly unusual black streaks. His eyes were blue. He looked as Egyptian as his father. The prince gave a huge smile,

"Hold this, King's Mother, it's getting a little heavy!"

As Khaemwaset was lowered into his mother's arms, he struggled to get as close to her warm body as he could. A wave of love, true maternal love, swept over the seventeen-year-old Istnofret.

"Is there something you haven't told me about me, Nefertari?" asked Ramesses. She looked away and shook her head.

"Have you lost every ounce of interest in me?" he asked bluntly. A shrug was his reply. "For goodness sake! If you don't love me, some fool without a broken heart can rule Egypt!" She grunted.

"Do you hate me? Have I done anything to upset you?" Another shake of the head. "What's up, Nefertari?" She looked up at her husband sorrowfully.

"I'm pregnant, Ramesses, and the doctors say that I will die giving birth to a stillborn child."

Ramesses knelt down to look at her. Slowly, tears of disbelief welled up in his grey-blue eyes. They cried together. Each stayed with the other. They tried to comfort each other. Nefertari wept every day, and cried all hell to the gods for separating the couple who were truly in love.

Istnofret didn't have to look after Khaemwaset so she had a lot of time to herself. One day she was given the privilege of a visit by Pharaoh.

"Istnofret!" he exclaimed. "I have missed you!"

The two hugged like old friends. "I need your advice. Are you willing to give it?"

"Of course, Ramesses. Speak your mind."

"I am thinking of building a great new city to house my imagination. In the delta, shining cyan, over the horizon. The city of Ramesses II. A worthy project for its funding…do you think? Or would it be too costly?"

"Not at all, Pharaoh. Your gold is as Tuya's dust. The Hebrew brickmakers will work on low pay, they are unskilled. I suggest you employ Prince Moses as their overseer. Build the city of your dreams, Ramesses. Anything is possible for you."

Ramesses smiled for the first time in a week. He liked people to believe in him. Even in this traumatic time Istnofret stuck with him.

"You are intelligent and you have a diplomatic way. For these qualities, Istnofret, I will always hold a deep respect for you."

Istnofret smiled next. Although she was unaware of it, these words of his were to strike true in the cruellest of ways.

The building work started with haste on a maiden site in the Nile Delta. All had secretly guessed that Ramesses would make this city the capital. None dared to approach the godlike figure. One day he tried to forget his sorrow and survey the work.

He called to Moses to ask how it was going. Moses dared not lie to Pharaoh but Ramesses would not approve of the truth. The prince gulped. He trod across the lovely grass nervously.

Ramesses asked what was wrong. He suspected nothing. Moses dared to complain, implying that a strike could well occur.

Moses paused to let this all sink in. The desired effect was not achieved. It didn't take Ramesses long to conjure up a reply based on fact. He suggested working them to exhaustion to keep them from causing a nuisance. He made a new order, that all brickmakers must find the brick materials as well as mixing them, making them, setting them, moving them and building with them.

Prince Moses' sweet Hebrew features sank rapidly. He knew of Pharaoh's wrath. He knew not to question it. He had tried to be the saviour of his people and ended up being the killer of them. He dropped his head and walked through the forest of green grass back to his companions.

He announced that he had news. The Hebrew people began to surround him so he stood on fresh haystacks brought in by the Egyptians.

The young and old looked up at Moses' bright skin and hopeful eyes, and for a moment thought he must be their saviour. He conjured up courage once again and spoke clearly, facing the sky. The Hebrews looked to Moses with a light in their eyes—the light the Egyptians never managed to extinguish.

But the news was not good. The people couldn't believe their ears. Moses was a Hebrew, but he was brought up under Seti's disciplining hand in Mer-Ur. Ramesses was his brother! Who was to tell that they weren't in a conspiracy? None of the Hebrews could prove that he wasn't. This made them brave enough to hate the prince. They started yelling at him, asking him to use the fact Ramesses was his brother to help them. Moses told them that Pharaoh's word was final, so he was nobody to challenge it.

The irony of Moses' words would have been hilarious had it not caused so many tears. The angry crowd separated, each one squawking for Moses' blood but not one bold enough to get it. The prince walked, head held low, to the palace. His momentum was stolen. Suddenly, his thoughts turned to Seti. How Moses had loved him, and how Moses had hated him! He was always a passionate boy. He did not know how he managed to remain civil with his father, the one whom he loved so much.

A vision surrounded him—of being a boy once more.

"Moses," Seti had called. "Moses, stop challenging the way of the world."

Reaching out his hand, Pharaoh had continued.

"Moses. It has been written that the conqueror of Egypt must wade through a sea of blood to get it. I am not proud of what I had to do. Come, Moses."

As the prince listened to the deep-sounding voice, he seemed almost hypnotised to go. Moses didn't move. He let Seti's words blow over him like a silent sandstorm. The explanation was not good enough. Moses held his ground. "Come, Moses," he called once more. In a rage, Moses tried to keep calm.

"Egyptian blood *will* be shed!" he promised. "For the Hebrews cried upon the bodies of innocent children, and the imbalance *will* be set right!"

Seti had sighed. This son of his didn't know what he was suggesting. He was obviously tired or confused. It was indeed a confusing process.

He could not hate the one who saved him. Seti let darkness surround him. He vanished as quickly as he had appeared.

Istnofret sat up and played with Khaemwaset. She was looking after him briefly as his lady-in-waiting was ill. He was growing up quickly, his sweet blond hair was clearly growing.

She had told Tionia that she worried for Ramesses. Tionia had screamed, her blue eyes opened wide, and then she ran to the palace. Istnofret had seen how determined Tionia was so she did not stop her in her way. The wife of Pharaoh stayed behind to look after Ramesses' beloved son Khaemwaset.

Not long after Tionia left the house, a young man with red hair entered and bowed. Upon seeing Khaemwaset he stated how handsome he already was. He suggested taking Khaemwaset to a palace nurse before going to see Setiptah. Khaemwaset looked upwards and giggled at the sight of his uncle.

Istnofret agreed. The two different people talked as they made their way to Setiptah's office. The courtyard passed by, its vivid colours reflecting in the midday sun. The sacred pool of Atum shone. It looked so inviting that the two almost jumped in fully clothed. In Unas' arms was Khaemwaset.

Unas confessed that Butokhi had never told him about his real father. He pointed out how strange their family was. He was a soldier, she was a peasant wife of Pharaoh and their father was a scribe.

As they walked, questions cropped up in the young girl's head. Who was their mother? Where were they born? How come nobody knew of their mother? Why did their father give them up? Unas wanted to know the answers to these questions as much as Istnofret, so they went first to give the king's son to a reliable nurse and then to the local scribe's office to see if they knew Setiptah's whereabouts.

Unas looked around himself. Papyri documenting seemingly important trials were all around him. An old scribe sat amongst this mess. He noticed neither him nor his sister. He asked if the scribe knew the whereabouts of Setiptah.

"You worthless little runts. Why disturb my complicated work? People nowadays always seem to want something for nothing. Mmschs."

At that he promptly and rudely went back to work. Unas was not deterred by this disagreeable scribe. He had dealt with many people like this before. He jingled coins in his small leather purse.

"Money! Hah! I think you'll have to find more than that to bribe me!"

Unas and Istnofret looked at each other, swapping shrugs. The scribe started to mumble to himself. Unas caught his apparently meaningless mumbles.

"Mmschs… fools. Argh. Setiptah's closer than they think. Stupid youths, ciachs. What do they want me to do now?"

"Father?" Unas exclaimed. Setiptah continued mumbling, complaining that Butokhi used to be a poor quality servant. For this putdown of his beloved Butokhi, Unas drew his dagger. Setiptah gulped. Sweat began to drop between the wisps of his short grey hair. As Istnofret had secretly imagined, here was the way to make Setiptah talk.

"Who is our mother?" she yelled.

"Mos-Iye-Et…" he gasped.

"Where were we born?" demanded Unas.

"G-Giza…"

"Why did you leave our mother?" Unas continued.

"She was… getting old…ugly—you… you understand…" he gulped. Unas drew his dagger nearer.

"How did she die?" Unas hissed.

"They said…they said grief. I left f-for court n-not her and they…they found her…twenty-five…"

My boy found it hard to control his anger. He was shaking with rage. Still he managed to keep his hand steady on the precious dagger by Setiptah's aged neck.

Setiptah found himself leaning backwards on his hands. He would do anything to free himself of his comeuppance.

"Why did you leave us? Why?" Unas continued.

"Youth. Pah. I never wanted you, and I never wanted your mother."

That was it. Unas lunged towards his father with the thirst for blood and skill of a fully trained soldier. As the iron sank shallowly into Setiptah's throat, something grabbed at Unas' feet. It prevented him from moving further forward. To Setiptah's horror, Unas dragged the dagger diagonally from his throat to his chest.

Setiptah's screams could be heard for miles around.

"You LEECH! You'll be devoured for this!" yelled the guard at Unas' feet. A strong other hand gripped the dagger. It pulled the dagger away from Unas' sweaty grip. Unas tried to strike the guard. The blow was parried. A hard elbow in the ribs was his reward for the effort.

Istnofret screamed. The guard grabbed her. Her breaths were short. She tried to remain calm. The gruesome weapon was less than a palm's length away.

Unas delivered a high kick. The guard was caught straight on the neck and knocked harshly to the floor. Still the guard gripped toughly to the dripping dagger. Unas stamped on the guard's stomach. This winded him almost completely. The guard saw his chance. He struck out with confidence at the lower right part of Unas' calf. The cruel hit bit into Unas' tensed muscle. Uttering a sharp cry, Unas fell to the floor which was now covered in his father's blood. Unable to stand, the soldier screamed in agony as the guard stood triumphant with the disgusting weapon. He held it quite close by his chest at a vertical angle. Istnofret saw her opportunity. She pushed his head and neck forwards with all her earthly might. With the dagger facing him, the guard could do nothing. His body hit the ground. A great crunch sounded as his spine was split in two.

The documents were illegible. Blood streamed through the room. Unas stared. Istnofret stared. Istnofret let Unas take hold of her shoulders. They left the office. They left Setiptah. They left him to breathe nothing in but his own blood. They left him in a room with a corpse. They left him to die.

Istnofret told the judges the truth. They were quick to realise it. They were confident they'd be set free. They only spent three nights in prison. The judge declared that both killings were justified, one in self-defence and one in honour. He smiled as he told the two they were free to go.

Istnofret was expecting Tionia to be fussing over her when she returned. Istnofret collected Khaemwaset. Of course, she had to overpay the nurse. But when she got home she found herself alone. Tionia hadn't returned herself from the palace.

Istnofret sat. She drummed her fingers. She wasn't clever enough then to work out the obvious and the inevitable. Istnofret was just a peasant-girl. Nefertari, on the other hand…

Tionia called Istnofret's name through the door of their home. She yelled something about life. Puzzled, Istnofret frowned. She thought only of Ramesses. Pharaoh had had a rather suspicious absence from the Hall of Two Truths throughout her trial.

"Nefertari is well. The baby is a girl. She has been named Merytamun." Tionia beamed through the door. Istnofret was amazed. This news was incredible. The heavens opened, and out poured this news. The one she loved would not be sunk into despair after all. She mumbled his name without realising. Hearing this, Tionia replied with respectful words describing his happiness.

For no reason there, Istnofret sensed that not all could be this right. There was a tone in Tionia's voice so rare. This tone was not pride. It was sorrow.

To hear sorrow in any form related to Ramesses felt too harsh for Istnofret. She walked to the palace because she had to see where this sorrow came from.

On the way she could smell the incense burnt to symbolise the gods. Her dress had become dirty and shredded; she had been in a filthy prison cell for the past three days. She did not wear any makeup or jewellery. She went barefoot. The buildings she saw there she felt were the most awesome she had ever seen. Too young to remember Giza or Heliopolis, they were the most awesome buildings she could remember.

Somehow the guards let Istnofret in. Maybe fate wanted her to enter. She only knew the way to Ramesses' bedroom, so she could only go there.

The engraved pillar lay behind her. Memories came flooding back. The door in front of her which Ramesses had opened for her stood closed. The ground upon which her feet lay was where Amon-Her-Khasimweh had carried her with much-needed care to the door. Gathering every ounce of bravery, she knocked on the heavy wooden door.

A servant's happy invitation to enter surprised Istnofret. She took it nonetheless. She gave her titles to the servant and formally requested to meet Nefertari, now Great Royal Wife and King's Mother.

The servant showed her a door in the fifth wall of the room. Before entering the room, Istnofret took a deep, deep breath.

Ramesses' luscious smell flew into her and calmed her effortlessly. She opened the weightless red door.

This room was a dark brown and muddy colour. The stench of incense was almost unbearable. A rug lay on the floor, covered almost totally by cushions and soft fabrics from lands far away. Upon them sat Ramesses and Nefertari. Istnofret noticed the sullen look on the queen's face. That was not just exhaustion. In a second; just a second, she knew it. This beautiful little baby girl was a miracle. Like this one, no more should follow. No words were spoken, though the tired queen could tell what Istnofret knew. She hung her head low. A frown followed; and after that a tiny tear tracing the way down her perfect face. Ramesses put his hand on Nefertari's arm.

Istnofret sighed. This was terrible news. Egypt may be plunged into civil war after Ramesses' death because of this. She blinked away her sorrow at the scene. Her sister meant so much to Pharaoh. She could not speak of what had happened to her here. She asked to see Pharaoh somewhere alone.

The priest recited an ancient blessing of Hathor upon all leaving the room. Istnofret left without looking back. She did not wish to see Nefertari's tearful face once more, neither did she check that Ramesses was behind. The door closed gently behind Ramesses.

She insisted that Ramesses had to know the story of Setiptah. But he merely sat on his elegant bed, with not a care at all. He quietly replied with the same. She had to know something also. So he asked if he may walk with her amongst the many rooms of the palace. *Surely not*, Istnofret thought. *Surely he wouldn't be seen in public with me? A peasant-girl?*

Pharaoh crawled across his massive bed like a little boy. He stood at the other end and waited patiently for his wife. Leading her out of the bedroom, Ramesses did not notice Istnofret jump as her heart skipped a beat. He grinned, pointing to the floor. He closed the door of the bedroom behind them. Istnofret realised that he was pointing to the alcove around the pillar, that place where she had hid so many times before. Ramesses sat in this alcove, then shifted quickly across to make room for Istnofret. The shadows covered both of them almost entirely. Some strange walk this was going to be. The peasant-girl sat so close to Ramesses that she became speechless. She could think of nothing but his sweet hot breath landing regularly on the side of her neck. When Pharaoh looked at her, she returned the very same look. It meant a different feeling for her.

Ramesses stretched out his left hand and took her left shoulder, rubbing his nose against hers. She still said nothing, as long as she could feel that breath she could not. How could he not love her if he wanted her like this? She did not know, all that she knew was her speechlessness. *Nefertari*, she thought. *Nefertari, Nefertari—she'd be upset to see her husband like this in a time of national troubles but...*

Ramesses seemed to know nothing but his lasting passion for Istnofret. He pressed his cheek against her neck and whispered something incomprehensible about Hathor in her ear. If only she'd have been able to hear it. So where she had hidden the years before, the girl gave in to Ramesses once more.

Istnofret awoke in her house, bewildered. How did she get there? Putting on a small white dress and forgetting to comb her hair, the peasant stumbled into the fire-room. She smiled as she saw her mother but frowned to see an elegant stranger drinking wine with her. She demanded to know his name. The stranger looked hurt that she did not recognise him. His ebony black hair fell in loose ringlets to his chin. He was young, and attractive to many. Not to Istnofret.

"Prince Moses," came the reply. The two exchanged glances, and they weren't pretty ones. Istnofret could sense the passion in this man. He had the capacity to cause great hurt, and she knew it. Moses lacked respect for this woman. The feeling of discomfort was inexplicable. It was mutual. So obvious it remained that Tionia felt the atmosphere and tried to calm the silent storm. She offered the girl some wine, but Istnofret rejected it. It was too early in the morning for her. Tionia stared back at Istnofret unmoved. Prince Moses proudly pointed out that it was in fact early afternoon. Istnofret shot Moses a look of contempt. Even so, it was still too early for her to be drinking. Moses returned Istnofret's look.

"One wonders what she might have been doing the night before. This living carcass was brought in by Amon-Her-Khasimweh very early this morning. It doesn't take an expert to piece that together…" he taunted her. She shouted it down. How dare he! Tionia made another effort to calm the tension.

"So was it Nubian or Oasis wine you wanted, dear?" she asked, all the while pouring out a strong white wine into a large, plain glass.

"But Mother, I didn't—" Istnofret began, but was interrupted by a hot-tempered Tionia slamming the drink into her stomach.

"Drink it!" she hissed with steaming breath, then turned to curtsey to Moses.

Istnofret flinched, every muscle in her body aching to cause Moses hurt. Before she had the chance to act upon her whims, her mother spoke. That was that, she'd set Moses off upon a long adventure, detailing his troubles up until the present day. Istnofret giggled. He was looking to the ends of the earth to find sympathy she didn't think he deserved.

Ramesses awoke early to hear Merytamun crying. Much to his surprise, he was wearing a different kilt even though he'd never changed… He shook his head, trying to work out how it could have all been a dream.

Nefertari entered the room. Walking gracefully to Ramesses, her fine linen moved silently over her delicate body. She sat upon the edge of Ramesses' bed. The Pharaoh looked up at her, a frozen image. Love.

Discussing Merytamun, they smiled together again. How beautiful she was. How similar to Pharaoh. Or maybe to Nefertari. What was behind that continuous gaze? Maybe no one will ever know. But it stayed there as long as both of them did.

Unas sat under a gorgeous palm tree to the west. Silently there he felt contentedness as he lay in the shade, occasionally sipping the cool, clear water of the Nile from his strong hands. He smiled. This life he could live.

A man who was bathing in the river lifted his head to gasp for air. He seemed about forty. There was some kind of dialogue between him and someone else—Unas turned his glance. There was the old man's wife. He could not believe his eyes. She must have been older than forty, but her beauty swept Unas from reality itself. Her voice became the ocean waves he had heard when he was tiny, her face the calm, calm waters.

Unas waited until the man, Toto, was completely covered by the water before limping over to his wife. Mud-brick houses passed them by. They were owned by the tomb workers near the Theban Houses of Eternity. Unas attempted to run. That was a bad idea. His leg was causing him much pain. Toto's wife sniffed. Tears ran down her cheeks. Unas knew that the only way to get to her was to sprint. He couldn't bear the emotional pain of seeing her like that. So he sprinted, and felt the gut-wrenching incisions of a thousand crocodile teeth.

The lady sat on a rock. Her head rested firmly in her hands. Unas, when close enough to sit next to her, did so. After much comforting and few words, the lady told him her name. She was Silver. Her eyes shot through him and shattered his heart. They were heavy with age and glazed with tears. And heart-shatteringly stunning.

It was later in that day, after the sun had set, that Pharaoh paid his queen a visit. This Pharaoh was here to ask advice from a lady he respected.

Tionia answered the door and curtseyed, with a massive grin on her face. She told Pharaoh that Khaemwaset was with the best nurse money could buy. Usermaatre Meryamun Ramesses gave a polite grin to the lady and walked through the humble house to Istnofret's room.

Istnofret sat on the floor drawing pictures from her imagination. As soon as she saw Pharaoh, her face went pale. She leapt upon her pictures so that he would not see them. Ramesses' anxiety stopped him from noticing Istnofret's clumsiness. Ramesses seemed confused about whether or not what he had told Moses was fair. Istnofret told him that she had met Moses. Ramesses laughed with his boyish loud laugh. His wife had met his childhood companion at last. How did she find him? Istnofret considered lying to her husband, but then paused. Her face would give it all away. She didn't realise that it already had.

Ramesses told her about his plans for a new city, to be called the City of Turquoise. The two exchanged tales like they should have done the day before. Pharaoh explained Nefertari's fight for survival following the birth of Merytamun. Istnofret explained her stay in prison, trial and release after Unas killed Setiptah. Neither knew much of Khaemwaset. Ramesses said that all of his brothers, Tuya, Nefertari and Merytamun, were in good health. It was then that someone's absence was noticed. One particular young man. Where had he gone to? Why? Why hadn't he been missed before?

Alarmed, Ramesses ran out of the house and yelled; "Has anyone seen Shanaar after the naming of the heir?"

Istnofret had a dislike for chaos such as those events, but she knew who would like it less. Collecting a small bundle of food and another dress, she headed for the palace barefoot as she had before.

The smells were so familiar that she could almost taste the presence of the royal family how it was before. The grand hall lay before her with musicians playing to an empty space. The guards had been away for some reason. The air was heavy. The girl needed some relief from it. In the corner of the room she saw the foot of a young man leave the ground. Curious, she walked over to him. He sat on a small wooden bench, gazing to the ceiling.

Istnofret took a moment to look at the paintings on the ceiling with the young man. They were of the finest quality, over to the left a pond with ducks and lilies faced her. She could feel the cool water falling from above. And to the right the stars, the beautiful stars, with a moon so real the round shape of it could be felt in the palm of her hand.

The man introduced himself as Mnao, the youngest of the thirteen princes. They laughed together. The prince looked almost completely different to Ramesses in bone structure and height, yet similar in some strange way. At a glance, you could not tell the two were related. Or so Istnofret believed. He told her of his engagement to a girl called Mnaktma'at. This was not ordered by the palace at all, this marriage was for love. They were both sixteen. Istnofret left the grand hall with a warm heart and a young prince leading her to Tuya's quarters.

This was a truly unique section of the home, with the tang of history in every corner. Tuya had lived in this palace for most of her life as the Great Royal Wife, so she owned a whole cluster of rooms each richly decorated and carefully ignored. Here was Tuya's touch! Things seemed strange and dirty through those doorways. She would have it so that dust confronted you in every object and on every surface. She would have it so that the pungent smell of the servants' sweat in years gone by followed you to the door. For here was the history that Tuya so adored, here was the taste of the past.

Cloaked in precious dust were items of rare furniture and great interest. Some engraved ebony tables seemed white to the eye not in Tuya's head. Everyday items such as clothes lost their valuable grey glint but retained their sweet ancient smell. Wearing lapis lazuli, silver and gemstones as they were made the lady seem glazed by ice.

Istnofret's eyes ran over Tuya's makeup desk, the mirror seemed more of a painting than anything else. There on the frail desk stood a stunning piece of jewellery, made of silver, inlaid with lapis lazuli and engraved with the titles 'King's Wife, King's Mother.' Here was the silver tiara which Tuya had only recently laid to rest. The old Headdress of the Great Royal Wife stood before her, patterns swirling round the stemline of the radiating silver. This jewel of an object inspired awe from Pharaohs and emperors. This tiara had been worn abroad to impress even the richest of rulers.

As Pharaoh's wife began to lean towards the mesmerising silver, a soft feather tickled her nose. She breathed in some dust. Without warning she sneezed all over the bright blue feather, scattering dust all over the floor.

Tuya heard the noise. She walked with utmost grace and elegance over to her desk. She appeared around a corner, in a doorway, a ghost. A curious ghost.

Istnofret and Mnao saw her. She was moderately dressed in a large black mourning dress. Around her waist hung a small gold chain, weighed down by the most fantastic ruby Istnofret had ever seen. She wore a fringed black shawl over her shoulders. Tuya leaned gently against the grey wall and stared at her intruders.

"I wore the Blue Feather when we marched against the Syrians," she told them. Istnofret was stunned. "Seti was on a campaign fighting the Libyans in the West. Although the Blue Crown belonged to him, he wanted me to keep the feather which I wore into battle." Tuya seemed indifferent to Istnofret's astonishment. The queen looked quickly at Istnofret and saw her wish in her eyes. She asked if she and Istnofret may be excused. Mnao left without protest. Istnofret noticed the moment he was out of earshot and spoke to Tuya.

"Deepest sympathies, Tuya." She bowed her head.

"No," Tuya asserted.

Istnofret raised her head in puzzlement. "No…?"

Tuya shook her head. "No, lady Istnofret. Shanaar needs to calm down before he returns to this precious palace. He will always care for himself. For this reason I am not worried. Wine?" she offered. Istnofret was stunned. She looked again to the strong-minded widow. She had to talk to her mother-in-law. It was not the time to put it off.

Tuya instructed a servant to pour out the wine. He did this without complaint. Istnofret found it exquisite yet could not drink much of it. Tuya waved her hand and demanded that lady Istnofret say what she had in her mind to say.

"Queen, my mother…" she began, afraid of offending Tuya. "Does it still cause you trouble to know that I am of humble birth?" Tuya put down her glass to touch her fine lapis lazuli ring.

"It is not right for Egypt to hold a peasant as Great Royal Wife. Lady Istnofret, for you to become Ramesses' Most Beloved would throw upon us more threats than benefits. It is not I who suffers the trouble from this; it is Egypt."

Istnofret found herself agreeing. Tuya was speaking the truth. Throughout Egyptian history, the sons of the Pharaohs had always been able to claim the highest of noble births, the best of the blood. If Istnofret was to be Great Royal Wife and King's Mother to Ramesses, his heir would have an unsteady grip on the throne. His challengers would demand reason for him to be there, this was not a time of crisis so why was a Pharaoh not with the blood of the gods sat upon the throne of Egypt? This could cause a civil war, more centuries of unrest and bloodshed or, ultimately, the downfall of the great civilisation itself. As if changing the subject, Istnofret questioned the queen about Setiptah.

"I remember him well," began Tuya, "although he was not

particularly out of the ordinary. Cunning little weasel he was…." She glanced quickly to the side. No, no more opinions, no more from the queen. "Dear Seti found him useful and hardworking. He became a scribe held close to Pharaoh's heart. He grew rich indeed for this."

Istnofret decided that now was the time to explain to Tuya. "Seti told me that he saw the face of a noble in me. I found Butokhi the guard. Butokhi told me that he had been paid to get rid of Seti's children. My brother killed him for the honour of my mother. I am the daughter of Setiptah and Mos-Iye-Et."

Looking down upon my baby I noticed her glowing. I returned the warmth I got from pride of her. She used my name. My baby kept my name alive. How I loved her for it. I saw Tuya gasping quietly. She tried to hide her mild embarrassment.

"There was quite a love story between your parents…" she told her, and then she continued to explain to my baby about me. Istnofret learnt from her. Istnofret was intrigued. A little while later, Tuya's face turned white.

"But… if you are a nobleman's daughter, you should be the Great Royal Wife! Nefertari obstructed Seti's flawless plan to make you into Great Royal Wife!" Istnofret smiled, with a look which explained her lack of frustration at this. Tuya spoke the truth always, this was indeed the truth for Istnofret. Yet Istnofret held no jealousy for Nefertari. The smile was gentle but enough to stop Tuya in her tracks. "You're in love," she finished.

The building work went on like Ramesses' dream come true. Ramesses saw it all, the colossi constructed, the temples built, the gardens planted. Only he did not see the turmoil of the Hebrew brickmakers. Wandering around this city he thought of Istnofret, the lady who had respected him and supported him always. She had fuelled the marvel. She had undergone a very slight personality change of late and Ramesses thought he'd seen it somewhere before…

The day had been relentlessly hot. Pharaoh had barely noticed the heat, so adapted to the Sahara dry season was he. The Hebrews, however, were not quite like Pharaoh. They knew they had to enjoy the weather while they had it, for the night would be ice-cold, African style.

"Put some effort into it!" yelled the Egyptian. The Hebrew people were dragging an obelisk into the air. If you looked at the bare sand below them, you would see blood, sweat and tears. Ramesses couldn't see the Hebrews. He saw only the obelisk, shining brightly in the midday light.

Ramesses took a walk by the Nile to think further about Istnofret. Had he noticed what she had not? He breathed in the musty air of his very own city—his creation.

At the bottom of one of Ramesses' colossi in the Ramesseum sat some young men, staring ahead. They were pointing at the statue's knees with curious looks on their faces. Pharaoh noticed what puzzled them and told them that the statue of the elegant queen between his knees was a statue of Istnofret. Still there, she is beautiful though half naked, carefully holding Ramesses' crook and flail.

Proud and handsome, Pharaoh stood in the path of the light. He found himself alone in the desert, where the Nile and the city of shining cyan were too far from the horizon. A familiar voice shook the heavens as Ramesses squinted for the brightness of the scorching sunlight.

"My son, Ramesses! Ramesses, I call you. The one who I named Ramesses, turn to me! Stand tall, strong bull! This will be of you demanded!"

Ramesses shook off the vision with a shrug. He felt his harsh face echoing the messages of the Sun. He was back in Pi-Ramesses. Grinning happily because of the speedy construction of the place, he sat down in the main square and asked for some grape juice.

Moses' heel had just left the floor of the main square when

his brother entered. Prince Moses retained the job of keeping his people in order. The job became harder as the days drew on. Ramesses and his Egyptians didn't care for the Hebrew workers. The Hebrews were certain that Moses was just the Hebrew tool which Ramesses used to convey his cruelty without feeling the consequences.

So Moses took a walk by the Nile. As he wandered into the soft, cool waters he felt them lapping at his feet. Nothing was so wrong with them; this wonderful creation overshadowed anything Ramesses could build.

Curious Moses heard a commotion near the outside of the city so he ran to see what was happening.

The Egyptian put his arm into the next lash of the whip. The middle-aged Hebrew man bent over backwards with the force of it. His blood turned the sand maroon.

Panting as the sand fell away from his feet, Moses felt the most intense anger he had ever felt. Gritting his teeth, he leapt upon the vicious Egyptian. As the lashes failed to return, the terrified Hebrew turned to look behind. His hazy eyes registered little of the scene. He collapsed on the ground in agony.

Moses screamed to the Egyptian, kicking him to the floor. Prince Moses had always worn his knife as a fashion accessory. Not so now.

As the dagger plunged into the man's flesh, he wailed the most frightful cry. All of the hurt he had delivered had suddenly returned. The frustration the prince felt for Egypt he took out on this man. Moses removed the knife, only to strike with it once again. The next time he speared the Egyptian's thigh. With the next time, he punctured the chest. He shattered the spine with the stab after that. It became so that Prince Moses was no longer killing the man; he was ripping the corpse.

People were running from the city to witness the destruction of a precious Egyptian corpse. It had been written that Isis found the fourteen pieces of Osiris to bandage them up. In doing this, she created the first mummy. This man's Isis would have a problem with his body cut up into twenty-five pieces.

Moses didn't hear the distraught relatives begging him to stop, he didn't hear the astonished onlookers' strange remarks. Prince Moses hadn't heard the man's final cry. He hadn't felt when the body stopped moving. Moses couldn't see the blood covering his feet, he couldn't feel his grip slipping on the lethal weapon which he continued to use. Moses didn't think of the idea that he was turning into a butcher and he acted on regardless of the threats he was receiving, the fact the man was dead and his victim was helpless. In this extreme fit of rage, Moses was oblivious to all but one voice.

"MOSES!" called Ramesses. Prince Moses dropped the weapon from his blood-red hands.

ISTNOFRET KHAEMWASET

RAMESSES LOOKED DOWN A SLOPING hill at the evil scene. He stood against the sun and folded his arms across his chest—the pose of a Pharaoh. Moses shook like a leaf. There was no hiding from that brother of his.

Slowly, Ramesses began to walk towards Prince Moses. Moses just stood therc, blood covering his legs. It was almost to his shoulders. Some had even spurted onto his forehead and cheeks.

Shaking was the least of the prince's problems. He knew the law. He knew the punishment for murder. Still he remained at the crime scene. Still Ramesses advanced slowly. When Pharaoh became close enough for Moses to hear him he spoke soothing, meaningless words. This is the way to calm animals. It works on humans sometimes.

When Pharaoh was no more than a hundred feet away, Moses fell to his knees. Blood dripped from his wavy hair onto his chest as if he'd washed his hair in it. Ramesses was set to win this one.

Suddenly, a dust cloud enveloped the top of the slope. The city gates disappeared in the dust. In a moment, hooves and chariot wheels emerged from the cloud. The prince saw, and jumped back to his feet. Men in armour and grand headdresses rode the lightning-fast chariots with style.

Pharaoh's police! Moses fled. He ran without stopping. Jumping on Toto's camel, he kicked it ruthlessly. It gave a loud and dissatisfied grunt. He kicked it again. It took off.

That camel nearly died on that journey. The chariots chasing the murderer toppled one by one as he galloped the camel through Pi-Ramesses. The very last chariot drove into deeper water when Moses was galloping through the Nile. The prince had fled.

Ramesses told Istnofret the next day. The nineteen-year-old girl found it impossible to restrain the laugh which cried to be set free. She was wrong! How wonderful! The prince could never cause any harm! Even if he dared to return, he'd face execution. She coughed. She told Pharaoh she was sorry indeed for the anguish this had put him through.

Two of Pharaoh's brothers were now in foreign lands. He could do no more to find them. They were not on good terms with him, and how he held regrets then. The likely events would not include Moses' return; he'd keep his wits about him and save his own skin. So Ramesses would never see his brother again.

Istnofret gave Ramesses the news first of all people; she was pregnant again. He knew it, by her personality change, but dared not say. Nothing could express their happiness.

Nefertari sat upon Ramesses' ebony engraved bed. She listened to the musicians playing in the courtyard below. Until now she had not known the meaning of the word unpleasant. The

Perfect One seemed disturbed.

Weapons had always existed, they were always used, but she only saw them now and they made her upset. To kill another would be… She thought killing another would be for some mother out there as traumatic as it would be for her if someone prised her baby from her careful hold and slew her. Whether in this world or the next, the mother would suffer equally. Nefertari knew she would, looking down upon her precious daughter whether she be six or sixty the grief would be the same. Political and intelligent, the Great Royal Wife knew exactly what had to be known. She now had to sign her name on vile documents beside Ramesses'.

Ramesses had always been her anchor but she had never seen him like this before. She didn't know how to take it. The only work he'd ever done for the army was organising food supplies four hundred miles behind his father.

Was war right at all? The Hittites had decided their position on that question five hundred years ago, at the founding of their civilisation. The Egyptians had their own differing answers still, after two thousand years. The general rule was that, as one Egyptian life was worth ten foreign ones then it is right to wage a war or defend the country if it will mean saving Egyptian lives. The Hittite way of fighting was unanimously believed to be wrong.

Young Ramesses was brave now. Would he be brave when faced with the more experienced Muwatallis? Here were the two great empires of the planet; Ramesses', content with peace, and Muwatallis', content only with war. It was then that an excited Pharaoh entered the room. Without a word he kissed his bride. He squeezed her shoulder with more force than he realised. Nefertari yelped. Ramesses didn't hear her.

Nefertari shivered. Her mind couldn't help but believe that Pharaoh was being foolhardy.

The buffer zone was a belt of useless countries whose princes had sworn allegiance to Egypt in return for their lives.

Each year the Empire milked them dry with every material surplus to be given in tribute to Ramesses. The main use of the protectorates was to provide a space between Egypt and Anatolia which would not allow any Hittite force moving southwest to make a surprise attack upon Egypt.

However, Ramesses hated these places bitterly. The princes never kept oaths. Threatened with a force greater than theirs, they would surrender and become another empire's protectorates. When the princes did this, Ramesses was filled with a lust for their blood. "The next time I come to them I will not let them get away with it…" he muttered, but his advisors always called to his sense.

Nefertari couldn't believe that, had Ramesses been born a prince of the buffer zone, he'd have acted differently. After all, these states had no hope left; Egypt prevented their expansion. No armies were to be kept, for the suppressed anger might otherwise take Egyptian lives. The protectorate rulers hated their positions but could do nothing.

Imagine almighty Ramesses, armed with a shovel and refusing to give way to the fierce Anatolians in their thousands with no army behind him. The coward princes were people with no chance to show any sort of honour. Still, Ramesses resented them for their cowardice.

Tionia brushed her dry hair aside. She was to spend another sunset with her fortunate daughter. What a joyful sunset that was!

Two months later, Ramesses invited his entire family to celebrate Istnofret's pregnancy by the banks of the Nile. Istnofret went with Tionia and Unas. Tuya invited every one of her sons to the occasion, and all except two sons arrived. Of course, Pharaoh brightened the stars and made the scorpions smile by bringing Nefertari, who was delighted to hear about Istnofret. The royal family had requested the presence of

Merytamun and Khaemwaset. Merytamun could hold her head upright and sit without great need of support. Khaemwaset was crawling on his hands and knees.

When Mnao appeared, the lady with whom he walked turned a few heads. He called to Ramesses, in utmost glee, to announce that they were married. Tuya called to everyone to sit down in a circle underneath an old tree. Glasses were handed out, and beer poured into them. She decided to address each member personally and this she did. She spoke to Ramesses first. Then she gave her endless pleasantries to her triplets—Nibitki, Kitinib and Tinikib. They were all a year younger than Pharaoh. To Tikinib's right sat Prince Rikawa. He looked nothing like the rest of his family, being fair and weak. He acted calmly, like the water to the family's fire. She turned to Amon-Her-Khasimweh and gave him her good luck for finding the love of his life. He smiled graciously, yet confusedly. Tuya laughed as she spoke to her twins, Djemus and Mbotus. She gave them her regards. She then glanced to Prince Karatki who sat to the right of Mbotus. Karatki always seemed to be the sane voice in the family, in spite of his age. The youngest prince there, Tuko, was sixteen. Tuya whispered a good luck to him.

To Tuko's right they left an empty space. Tuya always kept an empty space to the right of Tuko during family gatherings and feasts. The Unnamed's Kha sat there. Of ten pregnancies altogether, only one child of Tuya's didn't survive. The Unnamed was Tuya's stillborn daughter. Tuya never forgot.

Tuya then wished well to Istnofret and Nefertari, at once proposing a toast to the future of the new life. Istnofret tapped her swollen stomach, then took another sip of wine.

The hooded strangers passed the old tree. The wind rustled their black woolen cloaks. They ran quick-footed, like criminals. A few harsh whispers were exchanged.

"Where have you hidden her?" one demanded of the other.

That one was then beckoned to follow his flesh brother over a stone. A hiss back was his reply.

It happened to be that Zipporah sat alone until the early hours in a cupboard-sized stone shed in the freezing cold. One lighted candle accompanied her, and the brief but daunting scratchings on the wall which Aaron had left her to think about.

"I AM THAT I AM"
(The Bible)

This pregnant lady got no such reception. Moses' death may result if the royal family discovered her and her position.

The sun rose slowly at first, then as the orange sparks rippled through the Nile in numbers it picked up speed. Not knowing the events which would unfold that day or indeed any day it rose regardless. Time and again we live in pointless, inexplicable fear but look—the sun still rises.

With the sun rose the Perfect One, from a perfect sleep. Her hair flowed like the rays of Re, undisturbed because the Perfect One slept still and silent. She was as innocent as the violet. Her perfect perfume graced the harsh face of Pharaoh as she stretched quietly. Young Ramesses awoke staring into the face of the Perfect One, which stayed beautiful. It stayed miraculous, for there was not a single fault through it.

The papyrus lay on the floor of the hall. Moses' story of failure could have been sealed by this papyrus. Zipporah had looked on, terrified. Aaron had spelled out Moses' vision to Zipporah the night before. Moses had to let the people go.

Ramesses knocked on Tionia's door early that morning to request Istnofret's presence in the Hall of Two Truths, the courtroom. The girl was still asleep, and when she awoke she dressed in the finest dress she could find, with long shoulder straps and delicate linen.

Istnofret walked alone to the Hall of Two Truths, where she herself had been tried for murder. She asked herself a million questions. Who was being tried? The thought of a mere meeting never once crossed her mind as she paced towards the courtroom.

The entire royal family attended. The Perfect One accompanied Pharaoh. Eventually all was ready. The family were sitting when the water clock stopped trickling. Only Ramesses and Nefertari knew who to expect. The gorgeous room held colours louder than words at that time. A red carpet stretched from the throne to the door. Someone discreetly set the water clock up to trickle again.

Moses was late. The baby kicked for the first time in that grand courtroom but Istnofret remained silent. Ramesses would have it so that even the baby Merytamun must be quiet.

Rush, tinkle, trickle, drop—the water clock went on. The tension in that room could be tasted. Just as the glances became almost too awkward, a hunched and hooded man stumbled in. After him followed a cloaked and hooded man and a woman, who lifted the hood from the first man's face.

"Moses!" uttered Tuya, stunned. Prince Moses did not utter a kind word to one member of the crowd. His face remained ice-cold as he crashed his almighty staff on the plastered floor.

Mbotus smiled, but soon stopped after receiving a look of poison delivered from a deadly serious Moses. It was then that Moses made his way to the throne. Ramesses looked down with the frozen glare which Moses looked up at him with.

Pharaoh bellowed in the traditional way. He wanted to know why Moses needed to meet with them all. No feeling seemed to touch his voice. Moses took his time before turning his back to Ramesses. This was a great offence—Pharaoh had asked him a question. Moses bent down to throw his right arm to the right coldly. He gathered up his strength to strike the staff which he now held in his left arm again upon the cold floor and bellow back; "Let them go!" Ramesses gave his calm reply to his brother's turned back. They bickered pathetically for a short while, until it became clear that Pharaoh wouldn't give in easily.

That did it. Moses turned around and threw the staff upon the floor. Before the family's eyes the staff became a venomous snake, wriggling rapidly across the courtroom floor.

Quickly, Djemus leapt for the serpent and held it at the upper neck. Rikawa and Amon-Her-Khasimweh tried so hard not to laugh their very effort seemed comical. Tuko and Kitinib didn't understand the joke, but when their brothers whispered it to them they were also struggling with the effort of keeping laughter in.

Pharaoh didn't laugh at all. He reached across and snatched the snake from Djemus' hand.

"Brother…" He spoke to Moses. "Half of us were raised in Mer-Ur with you! We weren't brought up blind! That old optical illusion went out of fashion ten years ago!" Ramesses waved his hand. The three Hebrews were dragged down into the court prison cells.

Pharaoh was at the trial of Moses when Istnofret gave birth to his third child—a little girl. The only one there at the birth was Amon-Her-Khasimweh. Tionia still swooned over him like a young girl.

Hours and hours passed. Istnofret slept. The prince decided to find Ramesses to make him name his newborn daughter on the spot. Unfortunately, this would mean waking him up. Amon-Her-Khasimweh was surprised to find Ramesses asleep during the day. When he finally awoke Pharaoh, the reply meant for Istnofret to name the girl herself. When the young queen was thinking of a name, something very unusual came over her.

"Name her Bint-Anat, after my sister Bintat."

Moses cried and cried and cried. He rattled his chains and thumped the walls and cried and cried and cried.

Zipporah cried. She couldn't see Moses. The prison floor was awash with tears.

Solitary and vicious if approached, Aaron did not cry. He sat in the corner of his cell trying to order everything mentally. This didn't work. Moses and Zipporah didn't give him a second of silence.

Moses was losing the court case. When Moses seemed helpless he became frustrated. When Moses was frustrated, he was quite a handful, even for three armed guards. This lion of a man appeared to be built of muscle and brain.

They all knew the law's stance on murder. Now even the richest of the Hebrews was to shed tears. Those days turned into weeks. Moses became a caged animal. When the prince saw an Egyptian, he felt that murderous rage well up past his endangered head once more. Moses was only twenty years old. He rarely gave more than a grunt to Gentiles.

Prison rule was strict. The prince was beaten for his bad behaviour. This crusade to crush Moses' spirit did no such thing, for the spirit was Moses himself. A piece of fruit, a bucket of water and a guard with a club described accurately enough most of those days. Once, as Moses was being beaten by two guards, the door stayed open. The other guard was dragging Zipporah into court. The couple's eyes met. The prince stayed calmly on the floor and didn't howl, scream or scratch. They were put together when the guards noticed how much easier they were that way.

Zipporah needed Moses. She saw through her pregnancy in a prison. Her body cried out for vitamins and minerals when she had none. She didn't know what to expect, which terrified her.

Days blurred into one another but Moses noticed that the beatings slowly began to stop. Luckily for the prison guards, they had not laid a finger on the prince's wife. Forcing her to go to court and speak was the worst of it.

One of those days they instructed Moses to rise and follow them to hear his verdict in the courtroom. Moses shook himself awake, briefly listened to Zipporah's breathing in her sleep and went, head held low, to meet his fate.

"You admit to murder, Moses..." the judge began, "and it was witnessed by many. After the murder, you cut the body into a total of...." He paused to look at his papyrus. "Twenty-seven pieces! Are you not aware of the laws of Ma'at? You, a prince, should have learnt and respected the law of Osiris! Mummification, Moses! Not only did you brutally end the man's hopes in this life, but in the Underworld also!" he insisted. Moses looked to the ceiling. Whispering broke out all around as a papyrus was shoved in the direction of the judge.

"By the hawk!" he exclaimed. "Nefertari offers you a pardon! All you have to do is swear by Ma'at not to harm another Egyptian citizen. That—and become one officially yourself. Repeat after me..." the judge began.

Moses screamed that he would not in the fiercest way possible. The entire room caught its breath. Even the judge began to lust for Moses' blood. The judge put on a serious expression to read out the final sentence.

"In light of your crime and disrespect, by Pharaoh Almighty, the Princess of All Women and the Royal Circle, this court finds you guilty. You will be taken down into the Halls of Darkness this evening and you will be made to drink poisoned wine. After your death you will be mummified...." Moses groaned loudly at the end. Mummified against his belief.

A loud crashing sound shook the courtroom. Next, wood splintered through the place. A rather ragged carcass holding a knife and wearing a kilt smothered in blood burst in holding *another* ragged carcass—almost dead, holding a knife, and wearing a kilt smothered in blood.

"Pharaoh!" cried the judge. Ramesses held the corpse of the

foreigner in the air by the tips of his slippery hair.

"Cancel all proceedings! I have caught the man who viciously tore Egyptian flesh that day! Does he not look similar to Moses? Does he not *smell* similar to Moses? Was I not closer to him than any other person in this courtroom?" bellowed Pharaoh.

"All hail Usermaatre!" yelled the judge, rapidly freeing Moses.

Hands in the air, Istnofret burst into tears. The miserable grey atmosphere was orbiting her as if she was drunk. Moses would hurt her. Moses would hurt her. Moses had returned. Moses was free. Moses would hurt her. Moses would hurt her. Moses would hurt her with a disaster.

Prince Moses sat down with Aaron and Zipporah. I Am had given Moses another vision. In frustration, he told his brother and wife of what Ramesses had said. He told Aaron to tell the brickmakers to meet the next day by the banks of the Nile. Aaron and Moses wandered away from Zipporah, who sat underneath a young tree shoot on a rock.

It was then that she bowed her head and the clouds opened. I Am revealed himself, and she froze with awe. No more convincing. She believed.

Ramesses and Istnofret ran like hyenas clumsily through Court. Pharaoh explained, on the way, that the man he killed in the courtroom was not innocent, he was a Hittite spy. Poor Istnofret had great trouble keeping up with Pharaoh's massive strides. He, however, continued his tale about Moses.

It seemed Moses had gathered thousands of Hebrews by the banks of the Nile to witness something. Of course, he had sent spies out amongst the Hebrews. They were running to the courtroom at the time, when they got there at last they panted like dogs. The second they sat, a spy burst into the room. The young man fell on his knees, and screamed at the top of his voice that relief was present in the Two Lands.

Before the crowd of thousands stood Prince Moses with Aaron. Prince Moses had heard the orders, so he performed the miracle.

"So Moses did as the Lord commanded. He lifted up the staff and struck the water of the Nile, and all the water was changed into blood" (the Bible).

As the thousands gasped and stared, the prince made his way to the courtroom.. As he stepped inside, he was greeted by a hurricane of the loudest laughter he had ever heard. His brothers, the royal princes, were rolling on the floor, tears streaming down their faces. The only one with a straight face was Ramesses. Pharaoh sighed. This happened four times every year, and it was when the water changed direction. It was not blood, but water filled with red powder from Lower Egypt. Soon it would die down again.

"Let them go!" he demanded. But it ended as it had done before, with Moses walking out in rage.

A curious night followed. Istnofret sat on a stool in her kitchen, trying to understand her own thoughts. She could not remember someone else's words, which might have helped a great deal. She fell asleep right there.

"Urgh!" screamed Istnofret, as she fell backwards off her stool.

"Everywhere!" screamed Tionia. "Urgh!" A hideous crunching squelching sound accompanied a dazed Istnofret hitting the floor.

"So Aaron stretched out his hand over the waters of Egypt, and the frogs came up and covered all the land" (the Bible).

Tionia, in all of her disgust, explained it all to Istnofret. This had happened twenty years before. Sometimes frogs, attracted by the change in climate, drifted southwards in the river. She didn't know why this only occurred sometimes and not others, but she knew it wasn't a supreme rarity. The two ran to the courtroom, their feet slowly gathering up blood, tough flesh and guts. Istnofret glanced over towards the brickmakers houses in the land of Goshen. Not one frog graced the entire village.

"Let them go!" Moses bellowed. He was angry at the prince's reactions when he told them the frogs were sent by I Am. Ramesses, however, did not roll around on the floor clutching his belly and complaining that he'd choke on laughter. He had worse things than frogs to worry about.

In anger Pharaoh told Moses of his hypocrisy. He called himself a Hebrew, but, when his own life was in danger, he fled from them. He fled from his dear brickmakers. He lived the life as an Egyptian prince yet ungratefully threw it back in his family's faces.

Once again he left the courtroom with a red face.

"Why did the brickmakers not have any frogs?" inquired Istnofret, later that evening.

"Would you live in a bowl full of filth which lets the elements in, just for an intense lack of food and stink of livestock?" she retorted. Istnofret nodded—as ever, she was contented with the Egyptian point of view.

The scenery jogged up and down as they walked. One question remained: what was Moses going to think of next?

The Hebrew people were ordered to pile up great amounts of these hideous, half-rotten frogs. Never before had the people been so split! Half believed, half did not. Either way, those poor little creatures had incredibly short life spans.

~ ~ ~

When it happened, Istnofret was sitting on the floor, proudly cradling her new pet. It croaked. It was very pretty, with large beady eyes and moist, green skin. It was a little girl. That night, the queen got a nasty shock.

"Urgh... Aaaah! Help! Yuck! Urgh! Aaaaah! Yuck!" screamed Istnofret in sick-making horror. Tionia's scream set the houses alight, and set the ibises in flight. Surely this was the most gruesome of the plagues.

"Aaron stretched out his staff and stuck the dust, and it turned into maggots on man and beast" (the Bible).

As Moses and Istnofret (who repelled each other) made their opposite ways to the courtroom, Ramesses and his brothers were already there. Though the midday sun was high, the brothers only awoke when they tasted the tension between Moses and Istnofret. The prince sighed with relief. He wasn't being laughed at...not yet.

Rikawa stretched, and upon feeling the maggots underneath his clothes and seeing the sincerity in Moses' face, began to giggle.

Kitinib caught the giggle, and rolled over (which squirted maggot guts all up the painted floor) to see Moses' expression.

Ramesses awoke to what can only be described as colossal laughter and sat up (further inconveniencing the maggots) looking a complete mess and staring at Istnofret, who matched.

Istnofret had never loved Ramesses more then—she longed to be alone with him, talking to him just to hear his voice. She lived for him.

Rubbing his eyes, Pharaoh smiled. He explained that, as the princes assumed that he'd blame the maggots on his god, they all slept over in the courtroom.

"Let them go!" Moses repeated. Ramesses yawned, drunk.

"Go eat maggot-gut," he replied, brainlessly.

It ended with Istnofret hurling a bronze statue of Ma'at at Moses. On that note, she left the courtroom. To Tionia she reported that the maggots came and bred quickly, feasting on the bodies of the dead frogs. Also she reported that, unluckily for Moses, the statue had failed to miss.

The maggots soon died as the climate was not suited to them. Building paused in Pi-Ramesses as the Hebrews were made to sweep away the rotting maggots.

This time, Istnofret was visited by the Perfect One. As she entered the house, the sun shone brightly through the window-holes.

Nefertari's hair was black, and it fell straight to her hips. Her nose appeared petite. She owned a typical figure for Egyptian queens—she was fleshy, but beautiful.

The necklaces which she wore illustrated her authority, but surely Ramesses could kill her with the bat of an eyelid. Intelligent and beautiful, the Perfect One remained weak. She had never experienced the life of a peasant.

They had only just started talking—Nefertari wanted to find Istnofret's position on what was to become the Hittite war—when Istnofret gave a most frightful scream.

Grabbing each other's gowns, they ran at full speed to the courtroom.

"The Lord did this; dense swarms of flies infested Pharaoh's house and those of his courtiers; throughout Egypt the land was threatened with ruin by the swarms" (the Bible).

As Istnofret, Nefertari and Moses all approached the courtroom entrance at the same time, the Perfect One stepped aside. An elbow in the ribs sorted who was to enter first.

"And then..." guffawed Pharaoh, "he blames it on the flaming bush!" When Moses arrived, he was greeted by yet more torrents of laughter. He clenched his fists.

"Let them go!" he demanded again. Pharaoh replied sarcastically. He knew that flies came to Egypt every year, and they, like the frogs, were hardly rare.

This meeting ended. Upon arriving at his newly made hut, he found his wife in labour. The baby was a boy—Gershom. Moses was delighted.

Istnofret and Nefertari walked back to Tionia's house, talking all the while. The Perfect One was not contented with Istnofret's answers. It seemed the blonde girl's ideas were flatly in agreement with Ramesses'. Perhaps she was more infatuated than Nefertari had first thought…

Nefertari poured out her heart to Istnofret there. Those weapons she saw, they were hideous. The Perfect One found trouble with condoning these. Istnofret replied plainly that they were right if they were sparing Egyptian lives. Istnofret nodded at Nefertari's unhelpful guilt, not understanding anything which she said.

"Remember the saying," Istnofret spoke softly, "that in the season of the hyena the true leader of Egypt will have to wade through a sea of blood to save her." The Perfect One shook, afraid. A heavy heart, a heavy heart, no heaven for the heavy heart. Blood, dust, tears of pain…she saw the battleground already. Would dear Ramesses be killed? Killed for blood, dust and tears of pain?

Istnofret's mind flashed to Tuya. Great Royal Wife Istnofret…it had a funny sound to it. But while Nefertari seemed to be breaking up, Istnofret never would have.

It was then that the almighty kerfuffle occurred. Everywhere, dropping like the short-lived flies.

"The next day the Lord struck. All the herds of Egypt died, but from the herds of the Israelites not one single beast died (the Bible).

This was a ruthless plague; nonetheless, Istnofret felt no need to confront Moses. Still they laughed at him. Moses the father seemed the same as Moses the brother.

Pharaoh's fist pounded the door. Tionia flattered him with titles. She curtseyed. Ramesses muttered something incomprehensible and wandered into Istnofret's room.

Istnofret jumped as she noticed the ideal warrior stood in front of her.

"Diseased pig. Yuck. Herd of Amun, it was. Died, rot, yuck. Dead herd rot. Hebrews sweep rotting cattle to other herds. Yuck. Dead. And everywhere," he muttered. Istnofret sniffed his breath, and asked cautiously if he'd been drinking. "Irrelevant," he mumbled, and showed himself to the door.

It had been a long time since the young girl had been honoured with a visit from Prince Amon-Her-Khasimweh, and when he turned up on that miserable day she expected him to arrive with a long-awaited bride on his arm. Not so, but nonetheless he brought himself. Istnofret smiled at him, for she hadn't seen him since the birth of Bint-Anat. However, when the prince asked her what she thought of Moses he wiped the smile off her face in one accidental swoop. She thought she'd be able to forget her own prophecy in the presence of her brother. He asked if she might be afraid. The look in her eyes told the story for her. She couldn't avoid a lonely tear speeding down her cheek. The prince put his arms around her and held her like he'd never let go. In his strong arms she fell into another deep sleep.

"And Moses stretched forth his rod toward heaven: and the Lord sent thunder and hail, and the fire ran along the ground, and the Lord rained hail on the land of Egypt" (the Bible).

Istnofret felt like she'd leapt three feet into the air because the almighty crashing almost brought the roof down.

"By Ptah!" exclaimed Amon-Her-Khasimweh, "here comes

the rainy season!" Running to find something to shelter under, they stood in the doorway waiting to make a dash for it.

Screaming and panicking filled Thebes. All manner of Egypt's residents rushed around as herds of wild animals do in a panic, unsure which could be safer—collapsing buildings or giant hailstones?

Hand in hand, the prince and the queen ran terrified to the courtroom. Moses entered after them, wearing a thick black cloak which must have absorbed the ocean. Hunched and red-faced, he glared at Ramesses his foster brother. The sweet-faced and impassioned man attracted giggles from Kitinib, Tuko and Mnao, but not Pharaoh. His face stayed in pain, yet that was carefully hidden.

Tuya warned Moses not to blame this on I Am. Her face showed the utmost concern for this rebel. Yet if someone was to wander through her eyes, her mind buzzed with worry about Shanaar. The strong mother pursed her lips and waited.

Prince Moses lowered his head. He frowned. This man was maturing. Still, Gershom would never love the family of Pharaoh. A petty family argument, or a profound religious disagreement? Either way, Gershom and Zipporah would never receive the lives awarded to relatives of the princes. How obvious it was that Tuya wanted to take them in! How obvious that she longed to care for Gershom and his mother, to let the boy be a new prince! But Moses, assured in his position, accepted nothing more. He'd starve himself and his family rather than eat from Ramesses' table.

"Let them go!" he pressured Ramesses once more. But Pharaoh only mocked him in return. Moses turned red and screamed. He left after spitting on the throne. Istnofret cringed. Pain, Moses was to be the very bringer of pain. Tremendous pain.

Poor Nefertari, thought Istnofret. To disagree with Ramesses so strongly sounded extremely strange to Istnofret. The Hittite

Wars were closer now—further evidence was appearing from the protectorates that they and their Egyptian fortresses were being recaptured.

Egypt had disagreed with Hatti before, and the Anatolians had won battle after battle until a cease fire was arranged. For Nefertari to disagree morally with this impossible war was to make the war yet more difficult to fight. In five hundred years the Hittites had not lost an inch of Anatolia.

Ramesses did not dare to enter their minds, so violent and devious they were. It wasn't a pleasant thought, but he knew that the warlike ones had planned these attacks carefully years ago. They had decided that there was only one civilisation on Earth which could possibly beat them in battle. What a glory that would be to add to the new emperor's reputation!

Internally, the royal family of Anatolia was a fascinating one. The Emperor Muwatallis had a son, Uri-Teshup, and a brother, Hattusillis, who seemed to be fighting for attention.

It felt to Istnofret as if she had never fallen asleep, but she woke in the morning screaming, her face felt like it was on fire.

"Moses tossed it into the air and it produced festering boils on man and beast" (the Bible).

Tionia ran to Istnofret, having covered her own face. She gasped occasionally for breath. She instructed Istnofret to wear a white shawl around her face, and pushed her out of the door. Finally, Tionia had the opportunity to cry away the pain.

Pharaoh squeaked as a physician poked at a huge boil on his hand. All at once embarrassed, he smiled nervously and checked to make sure his brothers hadn't taken too much notice.

Luckily for his reputation, they had not. They were also being cared for, (painfully) and squeaking nervously themselves. Once again they had spent the night in the Hall of Two Truths. In this room, hundreds of men had been condemned to death.

Moses burst in, with an elégant black mask covering his temples and nose. Pharaoh laughed at him, asking him if he also had a case of White Delta Sickness. Prince Moses narrowed his eyes, insisting that the mask was given to him by the Hebrews as a mark of their trust. Halfway through his angry speech, Istnofret arrived. In a true stately and orderly manner, he did not turn around. This gave Istnofret an idea. Throwing her right hand in front of her, she crept towards the back of his head. She concentrated on the mask-tie at the back of his head.

"Let them go!" he demanded of Pharaoh. Tikinib noticed Istnofret's plan and kept Moses talking.

He began to turn when Tikinib gasped. Istnofret leapt, with the most tremendous leap she had ever performed, and her tiny fingers closed around the mast-tie. In full view of the princes fell Istnofret, the mask, and Moses' lie.

Ramesses jumped. Where was that shy little girl, too thoughtful to even tell her husband she even disliked her brother-in-law? The brothers laughed like never before. Moses left with clenched fists as he had arrived. A plague of boils and sores indeed, brought down upon the ungrateful Egyptians! The little blonde lady straightened her arms to arch her back and show Ramesses that she was hanging her head in shame. The shame, however, belonged solely to Prince Moses.

The soft African trees were thrown like feathers from one side to the other. The spray from the grass flew into Istnofret's face as she sat meditating, waiting for the sunset.

Khaemwaset was growing with amazing speed and intelligence. He had taken his first steps. Bint-Anat was a lovely baby, with light curls of black hair. Istnofret didn't feel like a mother because she didn't see her children often, but when they grew older she'd see them frequently. Ramesses was positively glowing but for every smile from him there was a tear from Nefertari. Merytamun spent her time with the Perfect One, who enjoyed every minute of her motherhood.

Unas still climbed the rope ladder of the military eagerly, with a happy disinterest in politics and an innocent approach to battle. Butokhi lived well, for Setiptah had given him a job and a son. The old guard was living of the surplus from both.

Istnofret felt privileged to know so many secrets. Unas, however, had told only Butokhi about Silver for her own protection. Tionia's religion was a secret. Toto and Butokhi remained good friends, but Butokhi's loyalty to his son was such that he could not tell Toto about his wife's affair.

Istnofret sat in the cold, cold winds and when she was alone, something horrible happened.

"Moses stretched out his staff over the land of Egypt and the Lord sent a wind roaring in from the east all that day and all that night. When the morning came, the east wind had brought the locusts" (the Bible).

A cloud of locusts swarmed all over the innocent gardens. Istnofret could almost feel the Pharaoh cursing. Those tiny creatures owned almighty stomachs. They did not stop eating until the crop was irreparably damaged.

Istnofret walked back to Tionia's house, hardly able to see because of the swarms. She was to be visited by Pharaoh's physician who'd be waiting there. The queen knew the story. Moses waited for the Hebrews' release. He blamed the locusts on his god. Ramesses laughed at Moses because he was blind to the future, unlike Istnofret. The pain on the outside didn't compare to the pain on the inside. Truly, Moses terrified the girl.

Tuya picked up the gold-rimmed mirror and inspected her fifty-year-old face. Once the giggling youngest sister of four, she was now the uncompromising guard-thing of Egypt. Shanaar ate away at her mind like the death grip that never loosens. Tuya did not usually cry. The Unnamed's death was the last thing to make Tuya cry. Sooner or later, the mother would break under the pressure.

She didn't find Moses' obsession funny. She saw him as damned, a murderer with a heavy heart, unwilling to repay his debt to the gods. Had she been a bad mother to him? She had always tried her best to love him, despite him not being her own child.

Was Shanaar really spoilt, or did he have a case for his actions? Secretly, Tuya wanted the co-regency. She wanted to help Ramesses to win the Hittite war. Only she could add the experience.

If Shanaar came to Egypt, he would be found. But Shanaar might never have returned. Tuya pondered whether to blame herself. Would she ever see her first son again?

It was then that she looked out of the window. It was amazing! Never in her lifetime had she seen such a beautiful but frightening sight.

Egypt came to a standstill, stood in front of what was surely Pharaoh's last warning. The farmers and craftsmen stopped groaning and covering their eyes to stare at the wonderful sky above.

"Moses stretched out his hand towards the sky, and it became pitch dark throughout the land of Egypt for three days" (the Bible).

Istnofret shivered, chilled by the darkness. Tionia lit an oil candle which flickered and came close to scarring her nose.

Tionia's life seemed curiously content. She was an orphan, whose father died when she was just five years old. She lived a peasant's life but never wanted to marry. She spent her life looking after Istnofret who wasn't even her real daughter. Life seemed harsh for her, but she saw the best in everything. Nearly thirty-six, she'd been good friends with Silver since the age of nine. Little did she know of Istnofret's links with the lady.

The two of them didn't need to say a word between them. Istnofret took the lamp and trotted gingerly down to the courtroom.

Istnofret walked barefoot on freezing stone. She wore a completely unsuitable wavy dress which was so thin it was almost transparent. As she walked a perfect raindrop fell from above and slid rapidly down the back of her dress. She shivered, and tiptoed quicker.

The frost-white entrance loomed before her through the merciful, light mist. Prince Moses was not there.

Staring at the ice-white surroundings encased in what looked like Siberian Ice and shocked by the room's beauty, Istnofret felt out of place. The pain remained in her, the fever had not left her. Still she was covered in sores. Still she felt unwell. The brothers might have needed her though, so she went.

Djemus and Rikawa sat in a corner together, laughing at a painting on the wall where the paint had dripped too much and caused interesting results.

Nibitki, Tuko and Amon-Her-Khasimweh were having a serious conversation about water supply and trade of animal hides. Mnao and Karatki lay on their backs, admiring the ceiling above. Tikinib, Mnao, Mnayakhama'at (his wife) and Mbotus were discussing religions together. Silent, Ramesses sat apart from the rest. How long was it going to be until Moses accepted his destiny? Like Ramesses was born to be a Pharaoh, Moses was born to be a prince! He repelled all heaven for…whatever it was that he really wanted. The Egyptians did not understand the prince. They didn't want to. How then, could Ramesses have done anything? How could he sign this contract without knowing the clauses?

Istnofret was always slightly afraid of so many men her age in the same room as her. This was partially because they were so strong. This is why when she saw Mnayakhama'at in unsteady candlelight, she headed straight for the circle she was sitting in.

In came Prince Moses. His hood was drawn well over his face and he held his candle inside the hood. It looked like his face was on fire.

"Let them go!" he bellowed again. The candle flickered to the beat of his voice. An awkward silence followed. Istnofret stared, mesmerised by the curious man. Ramesses raised his eyebrows slowly, unmoved. Moses' anger could be tasted.

"The death of the innocents, the death of the innocents, I Am will have his revenge upon the land where Seti massacred the children!" yelled Moses.

"Let them go! I beg you, Ramesses, adhere to his words and let the Hebrew people go!" she whimpered, grabbing hold of Pharaoh's fist. He shook her off.

Exhausted from the effort and the tears drawn from her prophecy, she fell forwards upon the floor. When she awoke, she was staring into the eyes of a physician.

The candles around climbed high. The physicians looming over were as temples. She blinked. Moses began to call the Hebrew people together, a great torch in his hand.

One physician muttered something to another, and felt her forehead. Istnofret's eyes opened wide. Moses addressed the crowd with arms outstretched.

A physician moved the hair from Istnofret's face. She very nearly fell asleep, and her eye became half closed. A murmur of hope spread through the crowd.

One of the young doctors inspected Istnofret's face to judge the extent to which the fever had taken her. She blinked for two seconds. Three goats were killed, and more were dragged by their hind legs to their imminent deaths.

Her eye opened a little as the physicians muttered quietly to one another again. Eager and quick, the crowd took sticks to dip in the blood of the carcasses by the torchlight. As Istnofret blinked completely, she fell asleep. The sticks, smothered in blood, were thrown around the doorposts of the Hebrews' houses, and the crowds went home content.

Rikawa gave Ramesses the news of what the Hebrews had done to twenty of their goats. Embarrassed, Rikawa had to admit that no Egyptian would enter the land of Goshen to punish the Hebrews because of the smell.

Huddled in pitch darkness, the Hebrews held hands. Hungry and cold, and terrified of what might happen if the Egyptians stormed in, they looked towards the only light in the room. That was the candle held by Moses.

Having learnt to trust the prince, their glimmer of hope, they obeyed him. Aaron and Zipporah sat to his left and right. Gershom lay in his lap. Moses spoke to the circle of followers. A murmur of disbelief began to spread about which was silenced when Moses clicked the fingers of his right hand. Through the doors and windows of the large hut walked four brickmakers, each carrying leather bags full to bursting with food. Each one carried a candle between his teeth. Smiles broke out all around the starving crowd as the food was blessed and eaten. They prayed, and then talked like the good friends they were. On that cold night, how warm this was. How warm. Moses laughed off the words about his asking Tuya for the food, and proudly explained that he stole it instead. Happy and hopeful, they ate their fill that night.

The fever took Istnofret away for two or three hours. The next hour was a dizzy limbo. One of the physicians prayed to Seth to destroy the evil in her. The water clock dripped. The five physicians never once left her side.

The next thing she knew, familiar faces were looking at her. Two of them were female, and four of them were male. Instinctively, she reached up to touch Ramesses' cheek. He smiled sympathetically.

Seeing Istnofret about to fall unconscious again, Amon-Her-Khasimweh took the initiative and began to speak to her loudly and endlessly to keep her awake. Through her dizziness, she heard the prince's words in the mist like the words of a god.

"Go take on the sky, Pharaoh loves you. Ride through the Underworld, Pharaoh protects you. Fight Sekhmet, Pharaoh will surround you." He repeated this over and over again. After an hour, the queen could sit up. After two hours, she could stand. After three hours she could lean on the prince's strong shoulders and begin to walk home. So the warning had been issued. So Pharaoh had remained obdurate. So Istnofret had cried and screamed in vain to try to persuade him.

"The Israelites went and did all that the Lord had commanded Moses and Aaron; and by midnight the Lord had struck down every firstborn in Egypt, from the firstborn of Pharaoh on his throne to the firstborn of the captive in the dungeon, and the firstborn of cattle. And such a cry was heard throughout the land of Egypt as was never heard before and never would be heard again, for not a house in Egypt was without its dead" (the Bible).

It was the first time the sun had risen in three deathly days as the eclipse had ended. The early morning rays of sunlight fell upon the white linen bedclothes and white plastered walls. Silver walked to the kitchen and got together a breakfast of fruit and bread for her husband.

In her mind was nothing but white; white for clarity, white for certainty, white for grief and white for guilt. The breakfast slid a little under her long, weary fingers. When her silver-white hair reflected against the white walls in the sunlight, she almost appeared innocent and perfect like silver. However, her guilt seeped through her wrinkled face. She held her head low.

A strike of lightning echoed throughout eastern Thebes. With the lightning followed torrential rain, beating upon the house's flat ceiling. Silver felt like a raindrop—before it dies it distorts everything around it.

Slowly, she walked to Toto's bedroom, hands trembling. Was he awake? Had she woken up too late? Would he beat her? Silver closed her eyes and stepped into the room, instantly noticing the pungent smell. As she opened her eyes she screamed and dropped the breakfast.

Toto's corpse lay sprawled all over the white bed linen, which served to sieve the maroon blood. His eyes were rolled back in his head. His left arm fell unceremoniously down the side of the bed.

Shaken, Silver ran. She didn't know where and she didn't know how, but she ran for what seemed like eternity. Free of her husband and free of her guilt, she ran and didn't stop for a long time. She ran to Butokhi's house out of pure instinct.

The white plaster of Butokhi's house was scattered with red sand which had stuck to it after the rain washed it. The rain had stopped but a creepy mist covered the land.

As soon as she entered Butokhi's house, Istnofret sensed something wrong. The air seemed heavy, even though the residents slept. The air bore down upon Silver, who couldn't cope with court life of any of the underlying feelings. She tried to shake it off, like she had shaken off Toto's murder as if it was of no consequence to her. Butokhi awoke to the sound of footsteps. He stretched his weak arms and legs, aching. The grunting guard Butokhi had never thought his generation would pass so quickly. But he was happy in himself. He stepped into Unas' bedroom and as he saw Unas he screamed and ran to his bedside.

Hearing Butokhi's scream, Silver squealed. She ran into Unas' bedroom, finding Butokhi in tears and Unas bleeding to death. Silver ran to his side and held his hand in hers.

"Silver," he moaned. He coughed and spluttered, blood covering his lips, until he finally died. His wounds matched Toto's. Butokhi bowed his head.

It was five minutes later when the distraught pair were running through court like buffalo convinced that Pharaoh had to know of this. When he discovered the news, he leapt to his feet and ran through the court, dragging poor Butokhi and Silver behind him. Silver found herself sprinting down corridor after corridor, her legs unable to move with Ramesses'. Where had her life gone? To the Underworld with Unas? In the palace nursery, Pharaoh was greeted by hordes of screaming nurses.

"Silence!" he ordered. "Now let me see what has been done!"

Istnofret woke up that morning when a physician burst into tears. Nefertari went over to the queen, but to Istnofret the Perfect One was just a blur. She wailed in complaint directed in Istnofret's direction. Istnofret rolled over to try to focus her vision. She'd heard her terrible cries.

"Tell me what has happened, sister!" she demanded. Nefertari could not hide it from her, and when she heard the truth Istnofret screamed to the sky "My babies!" Though her face felt nailed to the bed, she left it. She couldn't bear to wait to find out if her children were dead or alive.

Screaming and crying, she started to run. It was not encouraging to hear the almighty cry of bereavement rising from every corner that she passed. The young queen was no longer a shy, pathetic peasant. She was only maternal instinct.

As she sprinted through the palace of the court, her fever dissolved into the air. The pain of the boils and sores had ceased and her legs felt as light as the air itself. The pain was forgotten for the moment when adrenaline took over.

In no fit state to be standing upright, Istnofret entered the well-lit room. As Ramesses had been crowded by nurses, so was Istnofret as she tried to force her way through. Lightning struck. The rain pounded once again.

The masses of concerned parents and nurses herded like sheep around her. Their worried ramblings and confused tracks were of no consequence to her.

Eventually she took a deep breath and simply pushed aside the people there. But her foggy vision was sharp when she saw Pharaoh in front of her, stood in a corridor of parted crowd and cradling the blood-soaked body of Prince Khaemwaset.

ISTNOFRET
ONE

THE WORKERS IN THE GOLD mines ceased work for the week. That was the week of respect for the dead; as plentifully as gold flowed from the goldmines, tears must flow for those who advanced that day.

The earthshattering screams and cries of bereavement still rocked Thebes like the monsoon winds. It was in that week that the rains worsened, almost to pay their own homage and respect. The palace was washed from base to roof. The desert glistened with a sheet of water.

The wind blew everything onward as a reminder of the afterlife and the will of the gods. Cows stood under palm trees, carefully observing the dead among their own community.

Ramesses walked, each step a labyrinth, to the courtroom. Khaemwaset's stab wounds pierced him all through. What twisted creature could do such a thing to this tiny infant? His blood was Pharaoh's blood. The heir was dead. There was no other heir of Ramesses'.

The royal family sat upon ivory and ebony stools, ready before the meeting took place. The meeting itself consisted mainly of threats and beliefs. Moses upheld his belief that the murders were committed by the Angel of Death who passed over the Hebrews that night. Ramesses believed that the Hebrews merely murdered as many sleeping Egyptians as they could lay their hands on.

"It was the tenth plague of I Am!" insisted Moses. "The murder was carried out by his angel!"

"Murder!" hissed Ramesses. "You'd know all about that now, wouldn't you?"

"Why don't you share your talent for speech in front of the whole courtroom?" teased Moses. Ramesses had been beaten—he couldn't say that any louder. Moses wasn't the only one who'd broken the law.

Shoutings broke out among the royal family, angry at what had happened. This disguised Ramesses' embarrassment. Tuya interrupted Amon-Her-Khasimweh who interrupted Tuko and Nibitki. Prince Moses fumed.

"Let them go!" he screamed, for the final time. Ramesses sniffed, almost letting a tear drop from his grey-blue eyes. He called Moses a coward for murdering the little one and not fighting Pharaoh, which he should have done.

"Am I the coward, Ramesses? Am I the one too scared to face up to what I have done?" he pointed out.

"What have you done, Moses? I do believe I don't know..." teased Ramesses. Moses cringed. If he owned up to murder now, Pharaoh would be innocent.

Nefertari tried to calm the family but failed. The effort of Moses, once again, was almost comical. The Hebrews stayed, Moses left the courtroom.

Two months later, Istnofret sat near to the sacred pool in Amon-Her-Khasimweh's company.

"Congratulations!" he grinned, in the most genuine way that seemed possible. He hid his hurt. Istnofret grinned back.

"They say it will be a boy," she told him, glancing across at the hand which held hers. He replied dreamily, convincing someone that Ramesses truly needed Istnofret.

It was nightfall that day when the father sat down and cried. He cried for his virtual bereavement, and he cried for fear of his son's last few moments. Alone, the scribe cried, alone in his office the tears soaked the papyrus and ran like the Nile. He let out a tortured wail that grew into a terrible scream.

Istnofret was walking back to her house that night, candle in hand, when she passed the scribe's office she heard him whimper. She recognised that voice.

All of a sudden she was fourteen, love-struck, running carelessly to the local scribe's office. All of a sudden an inspired scribe was running back to tell her that he knew the man she was talking about. All of a sudden she heard herself muttering the promise of a favour—all over again.

That did it. She ran as quickly as she could, straight to the scribe's office.

This man seemed to be at the worst part of his life, nothing could deteriorate further than it already had.

She explained her story to the weeping man. He begged her for a favour—there was indeed something she could do.

His name was Amenemope. He explained that he was old and feeble—no longer able to look for his son, Rakset. He ran away from home aged twelve. Since then, his wife had died. He just wanted to see his son again. He begged Istnofret to find Rakset. She nodded and walked obediently back to the house, telling all to Tionia.

Amon-Her-Khasimweh nodded. Without a trace of disagreement, he agreed to help Istnofret to find Rakset. He teased her, saying that she'd need a strong man out there to fight off the hyenas. Upon seeing the worried look on her face, the prince threw his head back and laughed. The princes were afraid only for others; never for themselves. It seemed like a family policy—to only cry for someone else. The prince had been delighted to be granted absence from the battlefield. Ramesses gave him his very own office until the grand return from the battle. Officially, Tuya and Amon-Her-Khasimweh ran the country until Ramesses' return.

Tionia stumbled into the room where they sat, and began to blush by pure accident.

"Wine…?" she stammered, setting down three glasses on a table. When the prince looked up, she giggled nervously. Her eyes beginning to water a little, she ran quickly into the kitchen.

Taking a sip of his wine, Amon-Her-Khasimweh frowned playfully.

"She doesn't…?" he half whispered, head to the floor with eyes staring at Istnofret.

"She does!" came the reply, and the two fell about laughing.

With melted knees, Tionia grabbed for the first large object in the kitchen to keep her stable. It was unlike her to be so shy, but then again the prince was *very* handsome… While listening to his hysterical laughter, Tionia tried to cool her face.

Someone knocked at the door. Tionia walked towards it as if it were alive. She answered it with painted dignity.

A woman with glistening long, grey hair stood in the doorway. A delicate polish licked her cheeks and shone in the sun. Her eyes were faded by a veil of tears.

"Silver…!" uttered Tionia, in astonishment. The two embraced, reunited after many years.

Silver explained her story, how Toto was cruel to her, the affection between herself and Unas and finally the so-called Tenth Plague's toll on both. Amon-Her-Khasimweh and Istnofret appeared close to a doorway.

She told Tionia about how she did not see why she should

continue to live.

"No!" screamed Tionia, taking a step back. "You are a being of worth created by God!" she quoted. All of a sudden, she covered her mouth. Backing away from Silver, she walked into a large vase which toppled. Amon-Her-Khasimweh's face embodied his extreme shock and confusion. He found his loyalties torn to shreds.

"Please deny it," he whispered in his disbelief, "deny Akhenaten the Heretic, deny the Aten who is no more than air itself…." Tionia lowered her head in shame. To shout her views like that—something she'd never done before. Something she should never do again if she earned the chance.

Amon-Her-Khasimweh glanced across at Istnofret. Suddenly he noticed what would happen if he took action. Tionia's religion could cause a civil war, but only if he was stupid enough to let a civil war take place. For Ramesses would be forced to divorce Istnofret (the traitor) and execute Tionia (the criminal). No heir would remain for Egypt while the Hittites threatened Ramesses… Once more he glanced at Istnofret. He couldn't do it.

Silver and Tionia fell to their knees, begging the prince to be kind. Tionia wept, acting for her life. Amon-Her-Khasimweh complained at Atenism. Atenists constantly imposed their religion, or so he said, which caused great friction. Tionia replied for him to take note of Amunism.

"I'm wrong," he declared openly. Finally it had hit him that maybe the authorities of Egypt were wrong once in a while too. Maybe Tuya had been mistaken. Badly needing to cry, the prince ran away from Tionia's house that day a changed man.

A month later, the two had set out on their journey. Dust stretched over the Red Lands as far as the eye could see. It seemed that after this tireless travelling, Nubia could not still be far away. The prince offered Istnofret some water from an animal horn. She replied for him to give it to the servants behind the camels, who were indeed thirsty. Istnofret saw the servants and filled with pity. The camels seemed to get better care. After they had been fighting the terrain for nearly two weeks, they finally noticed signs of human life.

"Crocodiliopolis…" whispered Amon-Her-Khasimweh in hushed reverence. The monster statue of Sobek towered up to the sky from the centre of the busy city. His statue stood around the great temple, from which the great city had sprung.

A few lively people rushed through the streets. Most stared at these in confusion. Wives gathered to gossip around the wells and children helped their mothers to gather water. Nobles' sons sat together in the small but fantastic city school which bore the cartouche of Ramesses II over the doorway, underneath a stamp of the crocodile god Sobek. The houses were white and well looked after this side of the Nile. The other side was the side of mud-huts and peasants. Here the people were busy too, busy in the crafts and busy with their farms.

Along by the nobles' side of the city the roads had become perfect with their attention. The small troop of servants and royals arrived at last, at the grander side of Crocodiliopolis.

A scribe in the city apologised for not being able to hand out records of its citizens. Amon-Her-Khasimweh and Istnofret left politely. Istnofret soon had to sit for a short rest. The plaster-white city buzzed with life before them. It looked like a mountain—daunting. It couldn't have been too small for them then.

Istnofret grinned, tapping her stomach. She delighted in the idea that, in some way, she was helping the man that she loved.

The heat affected them both to such an extent that Amon-Her-Khasimweh's black hair trickled with sweat and Istnofret needed regular breaks. Finding herself sitting a lot of the time, Istnofret took the trouble of explaining about Bintat to Amon-Her-Khasimweh. He sympathised with her, and explained his own troubles he experienced when Seti died.

Istnofret asked him why he did not report Tionia to Pharaoh's police. He snapped at her in return, asking explicitly for them to leave the subject alone. Istnofret understood. Tuya had taught her sons that one religion was right, and all others were wrong. In the prince's accepting that this was untrue, he was accepting also that his mother was not completely correct. Because Tuya was Egypt itself, Amon-Her-Khasimweh thought himself a traitor.

An embarrassing pause followed. Ibises flew overhead. Wildlife squawked, leapt, shone in the tributary. For a short while, neither royal had a word for the other. The queen put an end to this by asking a typical question of an unmarried prince. He shrugged, desperate once again for a change of subject.

So the two went about the city knocking on doors, asking at shops, stopping at every well they saw. It took a week to get an entirely negative reply from the city of Crocodiliopolis. No man, woman or child from the city knew anyone called Rakset, or any possible relatives. It was nightfall when the two and their servants packed loads onto their camels to leave the place by torchlight.

It was the ninth month of the year and though the heat remained unbearable during the day, the cold remained vicious during the night. Strangely, the prince thought nothing of leaving a kingdom which might one day belong to him in Tuya's complete control. Every Egyptian knew that Tuya was worth more than most queens. Although uneducated, she still possessed a clear-cut intelligence and level-headedness despite (or because of) her experience.

Istnofret's camel stumbled slightly. She thought of nothing but Ramesses. He would be camping out in the open, riding around the troops with the other nine brothers to tell them the battle plans. The Blue Crown lay on the table untouched. Muwatallis was ready.

The servants felt uneasy. The two great powers of the world

were at war. They didn't know the intricacies, but they had heard many tales about the Hittites. No Egyptian liked the idea of Hattusa, capital of Anatolia, poised and poisonous, the viper in the valley. Padukhepa, Muwatallis' sister-in-law, haunted the balconies of the intimidating palace like a wandering spirit. Those who could afford to wore animal skin cloaks to keep away the bitter cold of the surrounding mountains. Padukhepa did so, in her hauntings. Padukhepa was fourteen years old.

A harmless desert snake hissed with anger as a sandaled foot fell upon it. Crocodiliopolis was now far over the horizon but the Nile was clearly within sight. Through Egypt there seemed no reason to stray far from the river. To Istnofret, the perfect delta was a lost memory.

Clothed in fine fabrics, Istnofret fell asleep after dismounting the camel. There were no disturbances to her sleep.

Nefertari awoke, heart pounding. Eyes wide open, she realised she'd been screaming. Putting a hand on her stomach which nearly covered it, Ramesses' face showed an expression of total concern.

"That will never happen," he insisted, sure of himself, "because look what I caught in the night." Nefertari squeaked with terror as Pharaoh pulled a wild cat in her face by the mane. After sniffing the anxious queen, it licked her entire face at once with an enormous, sandy tongue. It began to purr, but it sounded more like a deep growl.

"He likes you!" exclaimed Ramesses.

The sun rose again over the desert sand. The first traveller to stir was Istnofret.

Images fresh in her mind, she sat bolt alert. Nightmares threatening her, she panted away her fear. How she'd cried! How she'd begged to be woken from that fearful world!

Amon-Her-Khasimweh rose next. He ran an animal-tooth

comb through his long hair, washed, and then knelt.

"How weary is the waterless road! How can man walk when his throat is dry? Who will quench the traveller's thirst? The lowland is far away, the high desert is vast. The man thirsty on the hill laments. How can I order matters aright? I will find out a way to make them live and they will thank God in my name throughout the years to come. Future generations will glorify my energy because my foresight makes me consider the needs of the traveller," recited Amon-Her-Khasimweh, as he bowed his head. "In Your name, father," he completed.

Rubbing her eyes and shaking her hair into place, Istnofret managed to make a decent remark. She told Amon-Her-Khasimweh that Pharaoh had to continue Seti's good work. The prince replied by saying not to worry. As each pharaoh owned the same soul as the next, Ramesses had no choice. The best would be done, no matter how. Unbelieving, Istnofret challenged this.

"Akhenaten," she replied. There was no reply to that. They got ready for another days' travel.

It was midday when they sat down for a rest. They ate dates, talked and gave water to the camels. The day seemed unusually cool. They were lucky. They soon remounted their camels. Far off, through about five vast sand-dune valleys, they could see a beautiful oasis. Acacia trees and birds surrounded it.

The oasis was in actuality further from them than it seemed. The white-hot sun parched their throats as the camels slowly tripped onwards. Hours and hours went by, the valleys were truly enormous and the journey long. The travellers saw the stunning lake growing as it got nearer and nearer.

Miles went by, and the cries of the wildlife there grew louder. As the oasis stood untouched before them, the travellers salivated.

Finally, they reached the oasis—just before sunset the next day. They were weary from the journey so they set up camp under the trees. The servants splashed in the water and the camels bathed. Istnofret and Amon-Her-Khasimweh fell asleep to the sounds of the wild birds calling, the taste of chalky poultry cooked over an open fire in their mouths.

The figures cloaked in black lit a torch. The night was still. The prince was sleeping. Small, dark clouds hid the stars from view. It was time.

They stood in a circle and talked in low voices below their hoods. They were ready to strike.

The soft movement of the water hid the sounds from the stranger's heel. The royals slept so peacefully and still, they were not troubled by anything. No hints existed to sense. It was humid. The sand fell from the stranger's foot. It was sandaled in delicate and expensive shoes, fresh from Libya.

The stranger held a small torch away from the oasis, towards the camp, and moved to Istnofret.

Istnofret slept soundly. Her hair was too long and knotted with sand in it, her stomach large but covered by a cloak. The stranger knelt slowly over her, hands praying but then slowly moving towards her neck…

Eyes wide open, she saw the face of her aggressor. The stranger gritted her teeth and squeezed Istnofret's throat as if her life depended on it. Fear shot through Istnofret! Her hands caught in her cloak, they were useless. She kicked the assassin who squealed. Unable to speak, the queen realised that the hooded woman must be her voice.

Life drawing from her limbs, my baby became quickly weaker. The attacker knelt on Istnofret's bump. Overcome with anger, she managed to free her hands and punch her attacker on the nose. Before passing out, she felt the grip of death loosen.

The first thing she noticed was gentle and firm hands on her back. Next she noticed her consciousness slipping back. When she opened her eyes, she saw the face of Amon-Her-Khasimweh.

A servant screamed that he could see her moving. The prince lay back on the grass, drawing rapid deep breaths. Istnofret sat up and looked around. Torches were lit, and servants were staring eagerly at her. Each breath seeming deeper than the last, she got her senses together.

The servants told her that the assassin screamed when she was punched. Amon-Her-Khasimweh awoke and set fire to her hair with her torch. He caught one of the hooded ones standing around, but the attacker ran away.

Istnofret stumbled over to the breathless prince and put her delicate hands around his rough cheeks. She gasped, pointing out that he had blood on his face. Ignoring her remark, he panted loudly that Shanaar did not like nephews.

The servants said that the prince had overcome the hooded man, Nepicaten. His wounds came from that fight. He admitted that Shanaar had employed him and Mekityret to kill Istnofret. This was because Istnofret's baby was due to take the throne Shanaar so craved.

Nepicaten was decapitated after he gave a guilty plea. A servant performed this while Amon-Her-Khasimweh revived Istnofret.

It took a long time for Istnofret to return to sleep that troublesome night, terrified and uncomfortable. Her bump was worryingly lifeless.

The room lay plastered, painted elaborately like many other palace rooms. The servants huddled around a table in the centre, where two brothers stood side by side.

As two princes entered the vaulted white doors, the servants made way for them. The bodies lay out of sight.

Pointing and shouting, the brothers began to argue. The servants split to join opposite sides of the hall. Somebody called the guards. The argument turned violent. The argument intended to decide who should ascend to the throne.

One man fell slain over the bodies on the table. The white

sheet over the bodies turned maroon. The fight dragged the maroon sheet from the bodies. There lay Ramesses II dead, with Istnofret there by his side.

"No!" screamed Istnofret. She sat up, the gentle sounds of the oasis surrounding her. Amon-Her-Khasimweh heard her scream. He ran to her side.

She told him about her dream. Would it be Egypt's future? The baby wasn't kicking anymore…

"Go back to sleep," ordered the prince, brushing her hair from her face with his hand, "I'm sure you're wrong."

The weeks went by. It was an age before they reached the great town of Syene. In the middle of that age, Istnofret gave birth to a healthy baby boy. She called it Khameneptu. Looking after him was somewhat of a learning experience for her.

Khameneptu was tiny and bald. He had a yellow tinge to his olive skin. He looked very odd indeed, like something Istnofret had never seen before. He demanded a lot of those around him, and they grew to love him.

Syene was a thoroughly baked town. It was very rainy during the day. The air was damp and the heat oppressing. Corridors of sphinxes encased the entrances to the temples. Tropical trees grew in abundance. The days were long, the residents' tempers short. Sleep was the main occupation here.

The town was entirely free of Atenists. No one would refuse to bathe in the holy temple pools.

Every building stood perfect and clean.

The most popular jobs in the city were taken and given by the temple officials. Water carriers were rich as Syene was the nearest town to the quartz-rock quarries. Pi-Ramesses, almost completed, needed a great share of this precious rock.

Door after door was visited by the travellers. Two days in Syene passed uselessly. Istnofret searched by herself on the third day. She felt anger for her son, he held them all back.

Another door opened. It took so long to open that Istnofret

almost kicked it down. An elderly woman answered the door. She did indeed know Rakset, and could lead the girl to his house if she was paid to. Istnofret reached into her papyrus satchel and pulled out a copper coin. It was meant to be placed at the temple pillar but Istnofret judged that, in the season of the hyena, Hathor could wait.

The lady hastily exited her house. Istnofret felt as though she had solid gold strapped to her feet. She was a slow walker indeed but totally content.

Gradually, Syene passed by. The town was large but lazy. The temples looked elaborate but not imposing.

Nobody ran. The wells and pools were surrounded by couples and children, calm and sleepy but gossiping cheerfully. A few part-time farmers dazedly tended the fields by the Nile. No fights broke out amongst these people, for they lived on Nubia's doorstep.

Istnofret wanted to destroy something. She felt herself perspiring everywhere, she felt something heavier dragging her down. The queen realised she was sunburnt all down her neck. She noticed the climate was crushing her.

The time it took to get from one side of Syene to the other seemed to occupy a season. The old lady walked on. She remained oblivious to Istnofret, and Istnofret's discomfort.

They reached the house. Istnofret paid the lady, who walked off immediately. The queen stepped up to the door, knocking at once. She noticed a black shawl covered the door. A pretty little girl answered the door with tears in her eyes. The girl signalled for Istnofret to come in, too tearful to speak.

The room was grand indeed. Gold on the ornaments flashed in the sunlight. The family knelt on rare silks. Something lay on a gold-plated table cloaked in black. The family knelt beside this thing. Realisation struck Istnofret. Rakset's body lay underneath that black cloth.

The unlikely strangers sat on wooden chests in a circle. The wooden chests were decorated with fine ebony. Magnificent paintings covered the walls as plentiful as rain. Istnofret sat in silence, looking upon each stranger's face. Rakset had left three children—a boy, a girl, and a baby of just under a year old. To Istnofret's right sat Pasakhet, the mother, who wore a dark veil over her face. Eventually Istnofret persuaded Pasakhet to leave.

"Court… hmm…all right, we'll go," agreed Pasakhet, her quiet mind ticking.

The weight of the Pyramids had been lifted from their shoulders. The cool waters of the Nile washed the dirt from their bodies. Istnofret had almost begun to sleep when there was a jolt.

She jumped, realising the reed boat was being tugged to a halt. The babies began to scream. The sweet water licked the grass. The sun began to rise as they left the boat.

Amon-Her-Khasimweh left first, giving his hand to the young family and to Istnofret. He then helped ashore the servants who carried Khameneptu.

"Follow me," he ordered, striding confidently. A torch burnt in his left hand. It was the boldest gold that the servants had ever seen, but flickered menacingly against a night-like sky.

Even the babies fell silent upon noticing it, all were transfixed by the light of the flame. The smell of home pleased the royals. The smell of power frightened the children.

Time had trickled like the water in the clock when the prince found the right door. A sleepy old man entered. Amon-Her-Khasimweh greeted him, calling him by name. Istnofret cried tears of joy when she saw the happiness she had brought Amenemope. She cried tears of sorrow when they told of the sorrow she had to bring Amenemope.

Amon-Her-Khasimweh accompanied her to Tionia's house in silence.

"I love you, daughter!" called Amenemope to Istnofret's

back. She smiled inside so radiantly she made the prince's torch look grey beside her. She had returned the favour of a lifetime with the favour of a lifetime. The promise had been fulfilled.

A mauve haze polished the blackness of the sky. Still Tionia and Istnofret talked on.

For Istnofret's news was microscopic in comparison with the worldwide news. Egypt hadn't strayed under Tuya's firm hand, and Nefertari was leading the regiments of Egypt home. King's Wife, King's Mother Tuya had been preparing for a glorious homecoming—but she couldn't prepare for the unpredictable parts…

Excitement pulsing through her, the young queen felt she could not wait for Ramesses' return. She told Tuya, who coldly replied that the battle was worthwhile and ended in time. Too easy it was to be fooled by Tuya's nutshell.

Istnofret tried to draw but found her hands taking control of themselves. She tried to think of poems but she found her mind inventing words which did not exist. Istnofret was not in control of this all-encompassing happiness.

The sun flew immediately overhead. While some Thebans slept, others marched tirelessly. While some Thebans bathed in holy water, others sweated sickeningly. The sun relaxed Istnofret. She could not be active with the sun so intense.

Ramesses' Royal Circle called a small meeting. They were the local rulers who tried to help him rule Egypt. When one of them stopped to listen, he could not believe what he heard.

Drums were beating softly way over the horizon. They could only mean one thing. The man called out on the flat white roof. The messengers of Thebes ricocheted his astonishment from plaster roof to mud roof. Every man, woman and child lined the main roads of Thebes where they chattered excitedly and gossiped.

The drums began to beat louder. Istnofret and Tionia walked

outside the sheltered court. They were soon accompanied by an anxious prince.

"Ptah, they're not all there, are they? Ptah, my brothers, which one have you given away?" he mumbled, disturbed. The only thing that could revive him in his state would be the army's arrival.

The drum beat became deafening. The drums tore whole buildings down. They shook Amun himself.

All eyes turned towards the still palace. Tuya remained inside, the heat playing tricks on her mind. Faces turned anyway. The queen did not grace the balcony to receive them. Istnofret and Amon-Her-Khasimweh walked solemnly to the palace. The message of victory had not been a detailed one. The prince tripped up the white stone stairs. He ran straight into Tuya's arms.

"No!" she insisted, pushing him away. "You will suspend your sorrow. You will wear gold. You must do as I say, you have Scorpion on your shoulders."

Istnofret wiped the sweat from her brow. She tugged at her dress and put on some of Tuya's makeup. Istnofret slipped on some sandals, combing her hair at the same time.

"The drums are deafening, Your Majesty!" she screamed, "When may we exit the palace?" Tuya did nothing. They waited for an eternity, eardrums almost bursting.

Finally Tuya waved her hand. The two royals walked with utmost elegance behind the dusty Tuya. No servants followed their tracks.

The first chariot to enter the corridor of onlookers was an unusual one. It contained Ramesses' now-famous lion, Khepernebmaet. This means 'the form of the master of justice,' and was a devious name for one who had killed so many Hittites. He sat proudly, massive golden collar shining in the midday sun.

The second chariot followed soon behind, protected by a group of weary soldiers. It contained Prince Nibitki, wearing a red headdress and sitting next to an odd-looking girl. She was the newly named Kheperubastet—the daughter of a buffer-zone prince.

The third chariot contained Kitinib, who also sat with a foreign lady. She was Terak-Terak, the newly widowed wife of another protectorate prince.

The fourth chariot was tiny and surrounded by drummers. Tinikib was inside, next to his strangely renamed wife. He called her Tao-Mau, which means 'my cat.' She was another country's prisoner, freed by Tinikib who worshipped her from the start.

The fifth chariot took some time to arrive. At a leisurely pace, Prince Rikawa waved to the public. Gently, he smiled at the woman beside him who wore blonde plaits down to her waist. Because of her dominant personality, Rikawa named her Nebet—'the lady-master.'

In the sixth chariot followed Prince Djemus. He too had a wife—Mery. Her simple name meant 'beloved' and Djemus could think of no name more accurate.

Prince Mbotus was inside the seventh chariot with his wife, Hoteptiti. He sweetly named her 'happiness has come' and gave her more gold than he had ever seen before.

The eighth chariot contained Prince Karatki, who now had a Hittite wife. Her name was Shamateturi, in honour of the Hittite god. Karatki had let her keep her name in exchange for more gold for Ramesses.

Soldiers flooded the gaps between the royal chariots, and marched alongside drummers and army doctors. Their weary faces told their tales.

The ninth chariot arrived soon after. Inside sat Prince Mnao and his princess, Mnayakhama'at. They were full of great joy.

In the tenth chariot sat Tuko, with his wife Bitu on his left. She was from Anatolia, lucky not to be one of the prisoners of war.

Nefertari and Ramesses sat in the eleventh chariot, and a

great cheer went up as they passed by. Behind the eleventh chariot rolled the twelfth, with new wives for Ramesses. Soon they would be taken north and forgotten about.

The thirteenth chariot contained a masked man, tied up and held at knifepoint. It wasn't clever of him to betray, to fight against his brother. But neither was it clever of his guards afterwards to drop sight of him and lose him.

Behind that marched blindfolded prisoners, individually guarded.

Next there were two hundred drummers. Behind them were yet more prisoners, cornered by archers. Behind them, the disgraced regiments of Ramesses' army marched exhausted. The generals sat in yet more chariots, demanding that their regiments march faster.

The princes and their wives stood on the lower steps of the marble stairs leading to the grand palace. Amon-Her-Khasimweh, Istnofret and Tuya followed suit in joyful silence.

As Ramesses II and Nefertari walked up the palace stairs, all Thebes fell silent. Then, at the top, they turned to face the crowd. The cheer was unbelievable.

Nefertari walked three stairs down and turned to face Ramesses. At that, the whole of Thebes knelt to its god.

That endless night, Ramesses went to Istnofret. That endless night she fell in love with him again. When Istnofret fell asleep, Ramesses walked to Nefertari. That endless night, he slept in her golden arms.

Ramesses awoke before the sun rose. Something was tugging his shoulder. He opened his perfect grey eyes.

"Mother!" he exclaimed. Tuya fell to her knees by his bed, wearing nothing but her dusty silver headdress. Tears were running down her face but she was not crying. The Perfect One slept still.

"My lonely wait is over. I go now, I go now to Seti through

Osiris. I am happy he chose you and not Shanaar. Take care of the Two Lands. I will go now, forever, to meet you again when the time is right," she told him, as she died there in his room. The pale face hit the floor with a thud. Ramesses' shaking hands turned the lifeless body. All that Tuya wore now was tears.

Sacred inscriptions covered the room. She sat upon her golden throne. The others cowered below. Booming voices of damnation echoed through from the room next door. When she realised that she could not open her mouth she was terrified. After ninety days she felt something brushing her mouth which allowed her to talk and eat. She felt her face of solid gold being called to the room next door. Something dragged her.

She was not afraid, fear didn't exist there. But then she realised what was happening.

"Ib," demanded a servant, extending his hand. She found herself made to drop her own heart into it.

The servant dropped the heart. First it weighed down the scales. Next it levelled the scales. Finally the feather dropped by the floor.

"Neb!" she exclaimed with horror. Anubis stood before her, fangs showing. He stretched his arm towards the left, then disappeared. As she walked where she was invited, a drooling monster with the body of a hyena called to her;

"Mekhetkha!" but she ignored it. Amit may hate her soul, but Thoth did not. To the left she found luxury to the greatest extreme—every normal thing was wonderful. The trees called to her. Silt transformed the landscape, so it blossomed as far as the eye could see. Here in the Garden of the Universe, food was plentiful. The weather was always perfect. She moved towards the gold-faced ones.

Eyes open wide, she staggered, overcome. It took a long time to understand that no person here was unhappy. Even the servants in the fields had permanent smiles on their faces. The whole place mystified her.

She glanced up a hillside and saw a handsome young warrior glancing back.

"Tao berner ib!" he called down to her, face shining in the sun. He called her his sweetheart. She ran and ran until she found herself in his arms again.

Istnofret knelt in the temple with the rest of the royal family. Though mourning, Istnofret's heart still leapt when she heard Ramesses' voice. Istnofret and Nefertari tried to gaze at him in a discreet way but never quite managed to. Veils over their faces hid their expressions.

Ramesses took the flail of Pharaoh and touched Tuya's death mask with it. As if he was somewhere else, Pharaoh couldn't see the adoring eyes.

The smell was intense—one of flowers and burning incense. Tuya had fulfilled what she was intended to do, and gone to the Underworld to see Seti again as soon as possible. White pillars reflected the sunlight on their faces.

Istnofret considered her life in the temple. She was twenty-five. She still lived with Tionia. This arrangement suited them both. Bint-Anat had said her first words. Khameneptu was healthy.

Istnofret turned her mind to Khaemwaset. She had never been able to mourn him properly, too much passed too soon after his death. She hated Moses for taking Prince Khaemwaset. His mummified body lay encased in solid gold. He would be placed in Istnofret's House of Eternity when the time would take her away.

One of Ramesses' new wives was pregnant. Harshly, Pharaoh decided that when the baby was born it must stay in Thebes. The secondary wife must return to Mer-Ur.

Who was it that paid Mekityret to attempt to assassinate her? Could she trust Nepicaten, who knew that he was soon to die anyway? Nepicaten said it was Shanaar. If it wasn't

Shanaar, it could have been any one of the princes. It could even have been Tuya, seeking the throne for herself.

Istnofret felt such grief for Unas and Bintat. Both seemed to die needlessly. Both approached life curiously, only to be stung. The queen was careful if a little shy. Istnofret must not be stung.

Apparently, Nefertari and Padukhepa had sealed a peace agreement between Ramesses and Muwatallis. Istnofret knew that Nefertari would always favour peace over war.

Ramesses confused Nefertari. He said that he loved her, yet seemed to lust every woman in the Court. Istnofret noticed this but she didn't mind at all. As far as she was concerned, the Earth revolved around Ramesses. If Ramesses smiled the world could rejoice.

The building work at Pi-Ramesses was producing one of the finest cities of all time. Istnofret was honoured to have her image carved in stone. This way her soul would live.

Tuya lay dead on the altar. Queen Tuya had told Istnofret that she had Scorpion on her shoulders. The first pharaoh had set the traditions. Tuya reminded Istnofret to carry them through with pride.

Where was Mekityret? Istnofret couldn't grasp her deadly mistake, because veils obscure too much.

Mursilis knelt on broken pottery. His foot lay on Uri-Teshup's strong stomach, his dagger a little into the prince's chest. Uri-Teshup was pushed with great strength down on broken glass. A huge open wound in his thigh splashed blood onto Mursilis' kilt. Bruises covered the bodies of both men, Uri-Teshup's cheek was black. The prince's untidy long hair turned a darker than usual shade of red.

Mursilis called Uri-Teshup a coward. Uri-Teshup tried in vain to take a deep breath. He was slapped by Mursilis. He coughed up blood on Mursilis' hand. He bore his teeth at Mursilis, trying again to breathe. Uri-Teshup tried to wriggle away from Mursilis' foot, but the dagger sank deeper into his chest.

Mursilis stamped on Uri-Teshup's stomach and stood up. The red-haired prince passed out.

When Uri-Teshup woke up, he screamed. Mursilis had managed to cut off his left thumb in his sleep. A pot of the prince's blood lay on the desk he found himself sitting at.

"Sign the papyrus, brother..." Mursilis insisted. He held a crossbow which pointed straight towards Uri-Teshup's head. Dizzy and terrified, Uri-Teshup did as he was told. He signed the papyrus with a shaking hand, in his own blood.

"You are always the older one," hissed Mursilis, still aiming the arrow, "yet you have to be taught by me to be a prince of Hattusa. We will make the Egyptians pay—but *my* way, brother—my way!"

Tionia walked through the courtyard. The rainy season was clearly long gone now. The plants died around her.

The forty-year-old thanked the stars for letting her reach her age. She prayed to the Aten through Akhenaten to take her to the Afterlife calmly, without the death that was usually in store for Atenists.

There was no reply from Butokhi's house. After another hour, still nobody opened the door. Tionia became worried, so she walked inside anyway.

In the first room the flowers were withered. The offerings by domestic statues of gods were slowly rotting away. Likewise, the stink of the rotting food in the kitchen was unbearable.

The next room smelt awful. Tionia screamed when she noticed Butokhi's half-rotten corpse lying on his bed. His mouth and eyes were wide open with terror.

The next room smelt even worse. Tionia could not believe her eyes when she saw Silver dead on the floor in a pool of blood. Beginning to cry and severely shaken, Tionia knelt by the sickening body. It seemed that she had slit her own wrists.

Distraught, Tionia got up to run away from the terrible place. She picked up a bundle in the corner of Silver's room, which had hieroglyphics written in ink upon it. Crying terribly, she ran back to her home.

Mery awoke. The temperature of the room soared but she couldn't see a thing for all the smoke.

"Djemus! Djemus!" she called, leaping out of her bed. Prince Djemus was not there. Crawling along the floor, Mery began to cry with all the smoke in her eyes. Flames towered high around her. She crawled for her life to reach the door.

Screaming for help, she fell at the last part of her journey. The exhausted plaster from the doorway gave way. This landed on Mery's neck.

"Help me! Djemus! Help!" she screamed, but it was too late. She could not escape.

At midnight the moon flew hidden. Prince Amon-Her-Khasimweh sat, head in his hands, over his writing desk in his office. When he heard someone enter, he complained loudly. When he noticed it was Istnofret, he sat back to look at her, candle in front of his face. He warned her that there existed an assassin in Court.

The prince read the message on the bundle. It said: 'this is for you, Istnofret.' It was a woman's brain, soaked with the blood from her heart. This belonged to Silver. After a brief discussion which did not settle Istnofret's fear, the prince left.

"Good night," he insisted, as the candle blew out. She stood alone in the dark at the desk with the blood-soaked brain. She shivered with the cold. The sky was a moonless black.

A chilled scream rocked the mountain edge. Another murder in the street far below had been committed.

Dragging the floor, a cloak picked up what can be best

described as dead snow. The cloak itself was made of black feathers, and was far too big for its wearer.

Dew dripped down Padukhepa's nose. Her brown hair fell in lively waves down to her elbows. Her nervous blue eyes looked on.

The balconies of her mountaintop palace were her only places of refuge. The girl had no titles, was barely ever seen yet half of Hatti hated her. She knew that she could manipulate Hattusillis, so she did. She manipulated Hattusillis for peace's sake and for Egypt. Padukhepa cursed every step. Hattusa was home to a teenage population, mostly male, but she was married off aged twelve.

So much rested upon the shoulders of this fifteen-year-old. Making a Hittite emperor sign a peace agreement was like taking blood from a stone but she had managed it.

Her mind turned to the crafty Mursilis. What exactly was he up to now? Silence had surrounded the prince. This usually meant that he had done something worth being silent about. She thanked the gods for Uri-Teshup. His loyalty rested firmly on her husband's side, not the emperor's.

Hattusillis was twenty-nine years old. His face looked dull and his heart was dead. Both he and his brother intended to forget Mursilis' existence, but life didn't go that way.

When Padukhepa was born, Muwatallis' wife and the mother of his two-year-old son had a weeklong affair with his brother Hattusillis. Mursilis was their child, though they both hated him and he became the enemy of Anatolia before his birth. Muwatallis had Keshimuri sacrificed to the gods for this, but for some reason Muwatallis spared Mursilis this honour. Consequently, Mursilis could pretend to love his uncle. In reality, he hated Muwatallis for killing Keshimuri and sought revenge. His plot was clever. It looked like he stood on the emperor's side.

Padukhepa sniffed the rain. Mursilis must not be thought of; he was a dangerous and devious young man. She shuddered.

The truth was not pleasant.

High wind whistled round a brown wood balcony. Freezing temperatures plummeted to the ground below. She shivered at the thought of the scandal; the scandal over Mursilis which continued still. He was only fifteen years old, yet somewhere within him lay an unbelievably cunning ability to do harm. Nobody knew where he would turn next, and half of his actions were so evil that their details were shrouded within Hattusa. This black sheep was making himself known.

Where were Padukhepa's feelings in all this mess? Because of Muwatallis' anger at the time of her birth, she was married to a man with one hand. The right arm was chopped three-quarters of the way down with a blunt axe. Hattusillis was a hard-edged, cynical man who had no room in his in-depth strategic plans for Padukhepa. She found him as crafty as a cobra and about as attractive as a dead one.

Leafing through her own mind, Padukhepa tried to detach herself from the circumstances. She tried to become Anatolia, not Padukhepa. This she did with stunning ability. Only one flaw broke the plan. She knew it, but was making feeble attempts to forget it.

"Muwatallis wants another prince…" came a haunting but familiar voice. Padukhepa jumped, the victim of her thoughts having appeared in the mist behind her. The girl waved her hand; her brother-in-law's dealings with the throne didn't make her smile.

Hattusillis gritted his teeth. "You know what I mean, Princess…" he hissed, dew dropping from his hair. Padukhepa ducked just as her husband shot out his hand. It met hard wood.

"Go!" screamed Padukhepa, running down a labyrinth of outside stairs. She didn't know if he was following and she didn't know how far she'd gone. Somewhere miles from the palace she dared to stop. Somehow she'd got the energy to run there.

Padukhepa drew quick breaths. She had reached a small

peasant's hut, where the lighting was very poor and the residents away. In the near darkness she cried away her terror. Endless tears flooded Hattusa once again.

"As I kill more people, my eyes grow darker," declared a suggestive voice. The princess opened her eyes fully, and noticed that she'd fallen asleep. In that split second she looked up. She gasped.

Light played tricks on Mursilis' face. His deep blue eyes seemed to drown his emotion. Black and wavy hair stood out from his head against a pitch background. Mursilis looked and sounded very mature for his age. This was because he had to battle off cruel comments and implications, sometimes even actions—from a very young age.

Padukhepa jumped to her feet. Mursilis' evil blue eyes burned through hers. Padukhepa wanted to scream at the prince in anger for why he did not like her husband, his father. She could not.

Not sure what to say, Mursilis lit a candle. Padukhepa raised her eyebrows; he had black stubble. An awkward silence followed. Tugging at her black feather cloak, Padukhepa finally thought of something to say.

"Muwatallis wants Hattusillis to get for him a new prince," she mumbled, each word carefully chosen. "I guarantee you this," began Mursilis, in a lingering voice, "that Muwatallis shall get another prince by Hattusillis…." Looking into Mursilis' eyes, Anatolia flew from Padukhepa like a bird. "I hate Hattusillis!" she muttered, overwhelmed. "Forget him!" demanded Mursilis. And she did.

The walk seemed long and without reward. That was to come.

The Perfect One walked perfectly, her hair moving perfectly as she walked. Her perfect blue eyes couldn't have been more blue, and nothing held faults in what lay behind them.

Two beautiful people stood hand in hand. The beauty on the outside was incomparable to that on the inside. No words broke the beautiful silence between them. The desert at night lay vast before them. The night sky was yet more beautiful than them. Every constellation shouted quietly. This choir was something worth listening to.

Ramesses sat on the top of a sand dune. Nefertari danced to the top in complete elegance, to sit where her god beckoned. One looked to the other in the sweet darkness where no watcher could tell who was looking to who. One touched the other's hand to beg for protection. No watcher could tell who.

Pharaoh reached out his hand to touch a perfect cheek. At that moment he thanked the gods for letting him near something so faultless. Soft and painted skin met his warrior-like hands. Still not one said a word.

Silence filled the air between the East and the West. Only the royal couple were awake. Ramesses would have thanked Nefertari for her life and once again declared his unconditional love for her, but no words could express either. Nefertari knew her husband's thoughts and they comforted her there.

Never would that be repeated, this was Ramesses' life's best hour. Of all the numerous bravery in battles, of all the wonderful people he'd met, of all the lovely children he'd raised, none of it came close to this hour.

The Perfect One thanked Hathor. She did not know how it could be that the only man who had ever truly stopped her heart was the one she'd truly love. Sitting next to the great man was the honour of the gods, and raising his child the gift of them. But to be the subject of his thoughts, deeds and words day after day was some sort of a miracle. Like sitting to play Senet continuously for thirty years and not losing once.

Where did such perfection come from? Was it just there? Maybe it was. Out of so many unhappy and terrible lives, out sprang a perfect one. Ramesses now knew how Akhenaten had felt when he first declared Neferneferuaten Nefertiti to be the lady for whom the sun shines. Pharaoh would gladly have called Nefertari any one of the affectionate names past pharaohs gave their wives. What romance filled Hor-Aha at the beginning of Dynasty One when he called his wife Sweet-Heart! But words no longer told enough. Names were merely mortal.

While we may say 'love' so freely, no word can tell what it is. All attempts to describe the feeling fail. A few people might never know its true meaning. For Ramesses and Nefertari it was there, never to die.

Together in silence they thought only of each other. Both people lost track of time completely, because they were overwhelmed. Neither had experienced quite this emotion before. This had not happened for a thousand years.

Eyes were wide and inviting the sky. Hours had gone by in unaltered silence. Ramesses and Nefertari could not sleep, the feeling was too strong to sleep away. Not one would leave the other's side.

Bright and glorious stars shone in a magnificence which spoke quietly to one and loudly to the other. No moon crowded that sky over the desert.

Nefertari's perfect heart thudded. Still Ramesses was new to her, still she fell in love afresh every morning. Years had gone by but their love had only grown stronger. Egypt was their aim but they found their foundation in each other. Pharaoh looked over the Perfect One once more. Her black shadow showed the elegant silhouette of a perfect queen, painted with modesty.

The two had been in love for so long that on this sand dune all other people were forgotten. A perfect strong hand clasped a perfect weak one. Nefertari had realised her weakness three days beforehand. Mentally, however, she had never been stronger. Love swallowed them that morning as if they were a ship drowning in a whirlpool. The control over their life was passed to powers unknown to them.

Neither one smiled. They felt contentment to such an extreme that a smile would be a mockery of it. The perfect silence continued. Perfect love covered them so that they became it.

A flutter of light shot through the darkness and rippled silently on the Nile. A few birds awoke, but upon noticing the atmosphere remained silent.

Nefertari's crystal eyes shone in an innocent wonder at the world which they had woken up to, as if it was new again. The Perfect One's long black hair appeared in a complimentary contrast to the bright desert sands. More light struck the Nile to be rippled and refracted.

Ramesses' silent mouth opened a little in renewed surprise and wonder at the lady beside him. Once again he could see her, if only faintly, and was awestruck by her beauty. His delicate, unfitting grey eyes looked to hers in adoration.

Yet more light leapt upon the lifeblood river. Ramesses' heart moved his body at each beat. The supernatural love still existed in the silence, still astonishing them both and still solid. As the top of the sun began to appear the first few peasants awoke quietly. More birds began to move, but did not make sounds.

The Perfect One thought of how lucky she was. She couldn't measure her fortune. Of all the women in the world, she felt that she had the best life. Ramesses found her beauty to be legendary and her intelligence magnificent. He poured upon her luxury as if it were monsoon rain. This love swept across everything she did and lit the empire with kind fire. It turned the impossible into reality.

Looking back, the Great Royal Wife had no wrongs to correct and no people to thank. The Perfect One had lead a perfect life where she had committed no wrongs, she had thanked good people perfectly.

Taken over by physical exhaustion, Nefertari lay down in the warm sands. The man that she loved knelt beside her in silence, shading the newborn sunlight from her and cradling her head.

Warm sand covered her perfect back. It was then that Nefertari knew that she could not physically break the silence. She knew that Ramesses loved her, and also knew that she loved him in return. Looking into each other's eyes, they felt yet another wave of love sweep across them. As the first full appearance of the sun occurred, Osiris claimed the spirit of the Perfect One.

ISTNOFRET
RESPECT

SAND SWEPT THE DESERT SAND. Egypt was to remain always in mourning. The wind brushed the secret entrance to the late Princess of All Women's House of Eternity by Luxor in the Valley of the Queens. In this way the years passed.

By this time Istnofret had been the Great Royal Wife for four years. It had been a turbulent time indeed, with the murders of Hoteptiti, Shamateturi and Djemus. These were a mystery, likewise the name of the assassin.

The queen had had many children since the death of Nefertari. She mothered triplet girls called Kiatoa-Tasherit, Zekret and Khepertioniet. One son of hers was extremely premature and died soon after birth. His name was Ramessu. Istnofret also had twin boys named Unas and Amon-Her-Khepeseshef. The queen, now almost thirty, retained her beautiful bark-brown eyes. Looking to her old broken mirror she had seen her face change once again. Her skin appeared tanned permanently, her features no longer told of youth.

The oldest one, Merytamun, had the looks of her mother. Bint-Anat had long, straight brown hair and unnatural blue eyes. Khameneptu was now six years old and learning to write. Kiatoa-Tasherit, Zekret and Khepertioniet appeared opposites of each other. Kiatoa-Tasherit, although only four years old, was a replica of Istnofret. Istnofret did not know why she wanted to name her Kiatoa the Younger. Zekret looked more like Ramesses, in an interesting way. She had black curls closing in on an unconventionally pretty face.

Khepertioniet was the youngest of the three. As it had been with Istnofret, her name had more to do with others than herself. Her name meant 'The image of Tionia' and though her red hair didn't suggest it, Istnofret intended to honour her mother in this way.

Ramesses filled with such delight when a new son was born that he decided to name him after himself. For Ramessu to die the day that he was born was a very bad omen, and one which Ramesses in person presented to the gods.

Unas and Amon-Her-Khepeseshef were only one year old. Amon-Her-Khasimweh loved them as if they were his own and spent many hours with them.

Mer-Ur buzzed with life again. The place was filled with Ramesses' wives, obtained from a million kings offering a million false promises. In four years he had fathered twenty-six children by various short thought of wives. Each one he cruelly demanded was to live with him in the Court of Thebes. The nurses cursed at the sound of yet more motherless babies crying.

Istnofret never once questioned this. No Pharaoh she had known of had ever fathered so many living children, but this was the way of Egypt. She had intelligence for many things. One of them was to understand that she was not to question Pharaoh.

Great Royal Wife or otherwise, Istnofret could never occupy

the space left by the departure of Nefertari. Priestesses would awaken to the sound of tears in the Temple of Hathor still. Ramesses was building for the Perfect One a new temple in Abu-Simbel. It was to be called the Temple of a Million Years. It was to stand in Abu-Simbel for a million years as a symbol of this love which would last throughout. For when Ramesses had returned that morning with the lady in his arms, he was unable to answer them. No words crowded his love for Nefertari.

Istnofret accepted the way that Ramesses behaved around other women. She saw him as she saw Khepernebmaet, a fine creature controlled mostly by instinct.

Tionia had aged to her mid-forties. However, her dreamy sea-blue eyes had not. Still, she had a ridiculous crush on Amon-Her-Khasimweh. Still she had not married. Tionia thought of herself as a mother twice and a grandmother ten and a half times. For Istnofret was pregnant.

The twenty-year-old paced the balconies like a snowed-down dove. Hattusillis, Hattusillis, the name brought fear itself. After five scheming years Mursilis had indeed delivered his promise of a son. Hattusillis had rubbed his wiry beard and mercifully let Padukhepa go on the condition that she remained faithful in future. This she could not do. Mursilis remained her only escape from the evils of Anatolia and from Hattusillis. But what then was she to do, with another child of Mursilis'?

Muwatallis had a strong dislike for scandal along with a good nose for it. Unless Hattusillis would tell him the baby was his, Padukhepa could be in serious danger.

Why such hypocrisy? Hattusillis had many children by other various mistresses. One of these children, Rakesh, was almost as old as Padukhepa. Padukhepa hated Rakesh. Padukhepa believed that every civilisation had its purpose and secretly held a respect for Egypt. Rakesh held no such respect and didn't have intelligence enough to be capable of this. Hattusillis loved Rakesh. Every day he told her how beautiful she was, and how one day she would make for Anatolia a helpless ally.

Breaths hurried in an alcove lifted dust. Cold breaths hurried everywhere. The breaths which could be seen sounded quickly.

"Mursilis!" screamed a man's voice from another room. He'd lived through too much! The breaths were cold. He called an insult. Padukhepa's terrified face turned upwards. Her eyes let a single tear drop. She began to beg the Emperor for mercy. Muwatallis let an inhuman expression be Padukhepa's beacon. He drew a small dagger, declaring that he would kill her for the good of his brother. The queen, in her state, drew from her intelligence and asked if Muwatallis really loved Hattusillis, why did Mursilis exist at all? Muwatallis pinned Padukhepa to a wooden wall with a strong hand.

A face appeared around a door. A young man walked calmly into the dull room, declaring quietly that it would be cowardly to kill a woman. In a swift move, he leapt for Muwatallis' arm, forcing the dagger from his hand.

Through her tears, Padukhepa saw only blood. In five brief minutes, Muwatallis became a corpse.

The two brothers sat together in a room. In the dark they hissed at each other like vipers. Mursilis had got Uri-Teshup's signature in blood on a confession to Muwatallis' murder. And Uri-Teshup was going to pay for it. The throne would pass through his fingers like water. Or else, the Hittite Council might be presented with the document…

Uri-Teshup gritted his teeth. The whole ceremony felt like a slow death to him. The Kummiyan priests cloaked Hattusillis in the finest cloth in all Asia Minor.

Mursilis didn't notice how tense his brother seemed. He bit his nails nervously. Surely they could not crown Hattusillis without a disturbance! The pigs' entrails on the altar told him so. Frustrated, Mursilis intended to rip Hattusillis' flesh with his bare hands.

"What is this, O gods, that you have done?" He spoke under his breath. "You have let in a plague…" he smiled. Mursilis and Uri-Teshup narrowed their eyes at Hattusillis. "The land of Hatti, all of it, is dying… I shall have some harsh words with the foreign prince…" He continued to whisper.

At the front of the grand hall stood Prince Hantilis. The princes watched in hatred as Hantilis struck up a fire. Here and here only Mursilis was naive indeed. Uri-Teshup was terrified. The powerful one coughed at the smell. Hantilis seemed almost undisturbed.

It was Uri-Teshup's turn to bite his nails. Mursilis looked in the other direction. All that he thought of this ritual was that someday, someone would perform it for him. There was no fear in Mursilis' face. That was ridiculous.

Hattusillis threw the wax and mutton-fat into the fire. Hantilis raised his arms. His eyes burned with white fire, stronger than that he had just struck.

"As the wax has flattened and as this mutton-fat has perished, so shall he who breaks the oath and performs treason against the King of Hatti be flattened like wax and perish like mutton-fat."

Mursilis looked on with a weary smile. The new Emperor, Hattusillis III, stood before them. He vowed to avenge Muwatallis. The Empress, Muwatallis' chief wife, was not present. Until her death, Padukhepa would not own the title 'queen.'

The palace remained almost silent. Incense floated through it on a wave of darkness. Expensive and rare silks were hung from the ceiling. Such bright colours appeared grey in the dull moonlight.

One sound disturbed the quiet breathing. For a while no more followed. Then careful footsteps crept along the floor.

Silence sounded suddenly. A few words were whispered.

The next minutes were uncertain. In a second, pain dug deep through Istnofret. In that same second, a coward's cries warned the world. The queen became unconscious. Blood soaked through Ramesses' bed. He ran to the next room to check on Istnofret. The assassin received a strike so hard that when her head hit the wall it broke open. Shaking, Pharaoh shook his queen. Istnofret screamed. The fire of metal had burnt her cheek.

Amon-Her-Khasimweh heard the deathly screams and thundered to his brother's side. The deeds that were done were done. The prince was too late. If he would have seen Shanaar and Ramesses fight for the first and last time he'd have been helpless anyway. He arrived to find chaos, blood still pumping from the top of Shanaar's neck.

Ramesses II appeared in the doorway between his room and the one next door. He carried a very special load. When the prince saw the blood spilling from Istnofret like rainwater, he ran over to her.

"Done," Ramesses insisted. Amon-Her-Khasimweh felt his heart sink when he realised that he had not helped.

"These fingers," he turned towards Pharaoh, "they will even clasp a dagger for you." Ramesses nodded, accepting the compliment. Amon-Her-Khasimweh did not see it right to correct Ramesses in his assumption.

The prince walked through to the room of rare silks. The sight was horrific. With a flickering candle he could make out where a young lady had had her skull broken open on the wall. Random brains covered the floor and crawled down the wall. What he noticed was so shocking that he had to drag the corpse into Ramesses' room. Ramesses had thrown Shanaar's body into a corner but Amon-Her-Khasimweh tripped over the head on the way to Ramesses with the dead woman. He landed with an almighty crash, almost setting it on fire.

"Pa...sakhet...!" exclaimed Istnofret.

"Mekityret!" screamed Pharaoh.

When she awoke, pain seared through Istnofret. She looked through new old-fashioned eyes. The world seemed like one of stormy nightmares, glossed and blurred by constant tears.

Pain seared once again. Those tears were acid to the wound. What images flashed as lightning strikes in her mind! Blood still flowed. How terrifying this was, to endure pain like herbal medicine with horrible visions half untrue circling as eagles. More acid bit.

Another visit to the land of nightmares, another cold sweat. Sweat by the blood felt like needles rising from underneath her cheek. Fine linen bandaged the wound poorly, and to Istnofret it could just have been hiding a scorpion for the hurt that it caused her. Hurt continued to make her scream. Tearing pain shocked her. She knew that to avoid the shock, she must not scream. But screams rattled her head! Her head bore an endless expressionless face as if it were lifeless. Life came and went with the nightmares or pain. She did not know who stayed by her side. Whoever it was disappeared with the pain.

Nine princes sat in a circle. The rebellious teenagers had changed a lot since they first met Istnofret. Nibitki and Kheperubastet had eight children. Mnao had two sons with Mnayakhama'at. Tao-Mau had three children with Tinikib. Nebet and Rikawa had a white-haired son named Mkha-Sekhet. Tuko and Bitu had a son and a daughter. Mbotus frowned. The princes would not believe that his love for Rakesh was true. Mbotus loved Rakesh indeed, and believed her to be an almost perfect new princess for Egypt.

The princes sighed. How could he love her? She visited the palace once with a Hittite diplomat. Mbotus would make her stay as his wife but she returned to Anatolia, insisting that she would not marry an unsure man. She was pretty for sure. She was also brainwashed.

~ ~ ~

For a minute, Amon-Her-Khasimweh spent his time alone. He sat upon the stone floor with his head in his hands. The prince's heart beat for more than just life. A cold shiver surrounded him. He was a dog—loyal but not human. No human could be so dreadful as to even imagine his state of mind. Air was no longer the most essential thing, for as long as he breathed it his terrible thoughts continued.

The prince couldn't let go. He felt like sleeping for a thousand years in a palace latrine. Nobody was there to forgive his sins as nobody impartial could listen. His eyes flashed yellow. For a second the world was yellow. What treacherous thoughts swam in his troubled mind!

He threw his head against a wall; it wouldn't split. He would ask Ramesses to kill him but Ramesses may then suspect the truth. He tried to strangle himself but lacked the bravery. The adders didn't bite like he wanted them to. Such a traitor was not wanted by even Amit. Death wouldn't have him like he'd have death. Life, it seemed, still needed him.

Nobody may have suspected a thing. Such a burden would stay with the prince for the rest of his life. He crawled into a hole and slept, tears streaming down his face.

The months went by. Istnofret had a son who Ramesses named Merneptah. The scar on her cheek was large, though healed.

The palace priests noticed a terrible omen overhead the day of Merneptah's birth. Over the sunset, dying doves plummeted. Blood soaked the sand again. No one understood what this meant. No priest would dare relate this to the newborn prince, but every priest thought it.

Rakesh and Mbotus walked in the sunlight to their rooms in the palace. As if he were a priceless gem, Rakesh held the prince firmly. The end had begun. They were married.

Mursilis raised his jet-black eyebrows. His father paced the cold, white palace room, blind to Mursilis' ambition.

"What must I do to stop you seeing my wife!" he yelled in annoyance. The prince chuckled. Hattusillis was not strong enough to kill him. If he tried, he'd be dead himself. Hattusillis had aged so much. Bushy, grey eyebrows hid part of a wrinkled forehead. He was a monster dressed in robes.

Mursilis still had almost black eyes which shone dark blue in bright sunlight. He was ready to kill whoever he needed to kill. At the thought, he licked one of his sharp front teeth and smiled. The wind change brought inside the overpowering smell of smoking pork. This didn't make the prince cough like Hattusillis. He sniffed the air.

Hattusillis III frowned. Rakesh had gone. Who was he to adore now? He didn't know how many children he had. The sons would be gruff soldiers by now.

Uri-Teshup appeared in a doorway, long red hair tied in untidy plaits. The prince hid a liking for Anatolia, along with a devious ability to help it. The screaming rows began.

As the royal family argued and threatened, cold air struck the tiny princess' back. She heard a few shouts. Ignore them, ignore them. Something shone in the light. She gasped and hid it safely in the clasp of her fist.

The atmosphere was damp and heavy. Not much light could pass the worm-like clouds. The smell of smoking pork filled her sensitive lungs.

Her hair was long, straight and black. It felt soft and new. A pretty round face told of her youth. Her skin was of an olive colour, telling of her mother's birthplace. Hattusillis had forgotten her if he ever knew of her existence. What a blessing that was.

Her eyes were clear blue. Her jaw was wide and her neck delicate. What swam in her head? Not guilt like it would be for most people. She was too young to understand the possible consequences of her action.

The middle-aged trader was not observant enough to spot the presence of the princess by his cart. He thought only of the money he'd make after he delivered his load of meat and hides to the Egyptian palace. She slipped the sharp, shining object into the cart, which left for Egypt soon afterwards.

Ramesses visited Tionia's house in the dry season. He took with him Merneptah. The baby was peaceful in the arms of his father.

By this time Istnofret had graciously refused to live in the palace. Tionia was in her mid-fifties—an old lady by Egyptian standards. Ramesses paid Istnofret to make sense of minor political problems, sign papyri with his seal and appear with him on public occasions. Istnofret could afford to care well for her mother and make her house look beautiful.

Because of being the Great Royal Wife, Istnofret had the means to do what she pleased. She was taught how to paint. Her entire room burst with colour. Joyful figures occupied the wall. Ramesses stood over all of them, holding an ankh.

Tionia gladly looked after Merneptah while the royal couple talked. Ramesses explained to Istnofret that Amon-Her-Khasimweh had gone missing. This was very much out of his character.

Ramesses admitted that he had a mind to hate death. After all, had not death stolen Seti, Tuya, Djemus, Khaemwaset, Ramessu and his beloved Perfect One? He prayed that death may forget Moses, who he still loved, and Amon-Her-Khasimweh.

How unusual, thought Istnofret, it was for him to leave Court and the Palace without telling Pharaoh. Was this the action of a royal with Egypt at his heart? Of course it was—it just didn't appear so.

Nynetouckk and Uri-Teshup sat at either end of a dull stone table. Only their breaths disturbed the candle flame between them. It was dark. It had to be.

The shadow princess promised an offering. She waited impatiently. *A perfect match for Mursilis*, thought the prince, *in looks and deeds*. She was too young to frighten Ur-Teshup.

Cold annoyed both people there. *If only Uri-Teshup would hurry up*, thought Nynetouckk. Was he a true Hittite prince or not? A true Hittite prince would accept. A coward would reject.

Money for power, thought Uri-Teshup. *What girl in her right mind would take such risks for such an unusual gain?*

"I'll do it," decided Uri-Teshup, after some consideration. "First, I take power. Then you leave, Nynetouckk!"

The two shook hands. It was almost as if someone's death warrant had been signed.

It was nightfall a week and a half later when the cart arrived at the palace. Mbotus was to go to check on the workers unloading it.

The court peasants worked, piling great stinking amounts of filthy hides onto their backs. Half of them were paid to transport the blood-soaked and salted meat to the palace kitchen. They could almost feel the hearts still beating in the soggy masses of flesh. One of the peasants called Mbotus over to the cart to check on something that had been found.

"What? No…" exclaimed the prince. An arrowhead shone in the night. When he drew his torch towards it, he could read the words carefully engraved:

DEATH
WITH REGARDS
THE HITTITES

What was their game? Could they not allow themselves to be called weaker? Would they rather another horrific war? Who might have sent such a gift? The arrowhead was polished iron. What an insult! Hattusillis III refused to give Egypt iron before, claiming that it was a 'bad time for producing iron.' Their empire obviously saw the Egyptians as peace-loving, otherwise they would not have sent such a sarcastic message.

Mbotus couldn't sleep that night. He tiptoed across the house and awoke Rakesh, who slept in her bed. He explained the whole story to her. What should he do? The princess conjured up an ingenious answer—out of the ordinary, by any extreme—and Mbotus found himself nodding. By the time the torch in that house went out, Rakesh slept in two rooms at either end there.

Thunder echoed. Rain poured. Screams could be heard for miles and miles. An army invaded the palace. They had armed themselves with Nynetouckk's axes. Blood flowed as rain, washing away what had been before.

The heads of Padukhepa's children were kicked into the dust. There was no time to cry. Hattusillis held Padukhepa's arm with all his strength and ran through corridors littered generously with corpses and stairways soaked with blood to a chariot. Seeing them about to get away, Mursilis raised an arm to his bow. Surely this time he'd get it right.

His arrow missed! It sank into the wood of the chariot wheel. Hattusillis' wife shrieked. Mursilis threw his bow the floor of the dark wood balcony in frustration. Continuing rain pierced it through.

A blood-soaked, thumbless hand slapped Mursilis' cold, drenched face. In shock he stepped backwards. Uri-Teshup fought Mursilis once again there. This was as it always had been—useless.

Screams echoed. Blood flowed in a river down the palace stairs. The corpses lay either side of the corridor—each one with a white face and gruesome axe-wounds, terrified eyes still open. Nobody suspected this or Uri-Teshup.

Amongst the screams the brothers could not hear a fifteen-year-old girl chuckle. She grinned. Inside the kitchens and protected, the plan had been going smoothly. She'd get what she wanted yet. When she did, she'd be on a pedestal above every woman who'd ever existed before. She leant against a wall and dreamed.

Mbotus demanded that when he met with Pharaoh, it must be dark. Ramesses granted his wish. The prince went with him, alone, to the riverbank outside the Court and the palace. The fish stayed still in black water which did not.

The pleasantries remained brief. Prince Mbotus knew that they both had to see to urgent matters of state. He gave the arrowhead to Ramesses.

Freezing African nights stung them like mosquito bites. As if the wind was instructing them to, the brothers shook with this cold. Prince Mbotus explained the whole story to a stunned Pharaoh. He gasped in horror when shown the arrowhead. With a deadly serious expression on his face, Mbotus told Ramesses to try his utmost to avoid war with the Hittites. After all, was not their leading powerful, determined and strong? Was not their army well-trained, well-equipped and numerous?

Mursilis walked for miles and miles. He dipped into icy valleys. He clambered up less-than-inviting mountains. With an eye behind him, he knew roughly where he was. He watched the sky cloud over and the nights draw in. He stared at the stars he slept under. When he was a measurable distance from human life, he lay down in the dust and cried.

The messenger ran to the palace with an engraved stone. Those odd and quite ugly doodlings were obviously Hittite script—not Egyptian. They were translated as:

RAMESSES,

A NEW EMPEROR REIGNS IN ANATOLIA. IT IS URI-TESHUP, THE PREVIOUS CROWN PRINCE OF MUWATALLIS. HE IS NOT CONVINCED THAT EGYPT WILL KEEP THE TREATY. THEREFORE (URI-TESHUP) DEMANDS THAT YOU SHALL MARRY HIS COUSIN, NYNETOUCKK. OF COURSE WE WILL NOT ALLOW A HITTITE PRINCESS TO BE ANYTHING OTHER THAN GREAT ROYAL WIFE.

IF YOU REFUSE TO COMPLY WE WILL SEE IT AS THE FIRST ACT OF WAR ON THE PART OF YOUR COUNTRY.

Ramesses called Mbotus to his side almost immediately. Intense confusion followed. Ramesses called upon the Royal Circle. He even invited the high judges to speak.

No Great Royal Wife had ever been *divorced* as such before. Some had resigned from their duties and one-who-shall-remain-nameless had been exiled. The Hittites were demanding the divorce of Istnofret. Failing that, they would want her lowered to the status of a secondary wife. These were both public humiliations.

However, this matter concerned not just Istnofret. The ancient traditions of Egypt were also being threatened. How dare the Hittites attempt to force Ramesses to lower the status of the role of Great Royal Wife! This was culture being trodden on, tradition lost—something Tuya would have been disgusted by.

But what if he refused? Hundreds, possibly thousands, of Egyptian lives would be lost. The Hittite army was a sparkling killing machine with order second to none. Their weapons were produced on a large scale. They used the newest technology. Every mistake they made they learnt from.

It took all day and all night to make two decisions. Firstly, no matter what was to happen eventually, Istnofret wasn't to know of this news. Secondly, Ramesses had to put off the actual decision for as long as possible. Maybe the Hittites would grow kinder. No matter how unlikely that seemed, anything was worth trying in these testing times. Ramesses called to the gods for Amon-Her-Khasimweh. The gods replied in their own way. It was for the best that the prince remained where he was. A document was drawn up:

> **MY BROTHER URI-TESHUP,**
> **THE LAND OF EGYPT REMAINS WITH PEACEFUL INTENTIONS TOWARD (HATTI), (AS IT WAS WHEN) THE TREATY WAS SIGNED. IF YOU WOULD STILL (REQUIRE) NYNETOUCKK TO MARRY, PLEASE REVIEW YOUR OFFER AND LET HER STAY IN THE TWO LANDS AS A SECONDARY WIFE.**

Ramesses hoped that he could sufficiently bide time enough to make the Hittite royals think. He slept all day the next day. Nightmares flooded his short deaths. He cried for the Perfect One.

The situation was familiar. The uncrowned emperor lay bruised on the floor. His brother knelt over him with a dagger.

Mursilis had returned. No Hittite knew this better than Uri-Teshup. Again the younger prince had won the fight. He would not win this fight again. This time he didn't want the Emperor's signature. He wanted his head. Not content with presenting the signature to the Council (as Uri-Teshup had refused to pass the crown immediately to Mursilis) Mursilis intended to end it all himself.

"Anything!" coughed Uri-Teshup. Mursilis shook his head with evil glee. Finally, and without fear, he could murder his brother. He did this with relish, watching him in the hours it took to bleed gradually to death.

Only one man was left to crown in Anatolia.

Darkness covered the land of Egypt. A deathly silence shrouded the pretty Egyptian princess. Communication could be a terrible thing. She hid it behind her massive eyes.

Tionia's plaster-white house appeared grey with only the light of the moon reflecting from it. Darkness had a purpose. It held the Egyptians in a fiery death. Istnofret awoke with the shock of sensing a presence in her bedroom. Rakesh's oil lamp brought the painted figures on the walls to life. What was she doing there? She walked slowly to the head of Istnofret's bed.

"What's happening?" Istnofret asked Rakesh. Rakesh told her exactly what was happening. Rakesh had a prepared answer for Istnofret's natural question—why didn't Ramesses tell her? Because she was now a burden! She didn't *deserve* to know matters of state anymore! Rakesh left an upset and bewildered Istnofret.

Amon-Her-Khasimweh awoke screaming. He had had another nightmare. It foretold terrible danger from the Hittites. He was alone. The desert couldn't tell him he was being ridiculous. Only one thing filled his mind as he leapt back onto the camel and attempted to travel from one side of northern Africa to the other.

The wooden throne sat neatly in the white-out room. It had become rain soaked and worn over the years. Woodworm infested it. It remained tall and awe-inspiring anyway.

Mursilis sat on the old throne. His robes had got caught in the dusty holes. He smiled to himself. Nobody crowded the room. Could a heart exist behind those cruel black eyes? He wondered why a part of him seemed astray. Maybe it was the loss of his family… But that he did not fully understand. He still gave the world another grin. His mind continued as one of a winner.

The air floated sweetly that day. Mursilis would have gladly spent it alone. He'd achieved all that he wanted to. He'd become the Emperor…though Padukhepa left, and the children were murdered…

Nynetouckk entered the room to make the same request again. Mursilis had no reason to deny his half-sister. But he had isolated himself. Nynetouckk didn't love him.

A reply was found to translate as:

> **RAMESSES,**
> **YOU WILL NOW ADDRESS COMMUNICATION TO THE EMPEROR MURSILIS. ONLY ONE FURTHER (LETTER) REMAINS FOR YOU TO WRITE. YOU WILL WRITE THAT, TO AVOID WAR WITH THE MIGHTY HITTITE ARMY, YOU WILL MARRY NYNETOUCKK AS THE GREAT ROYAL WIFE. IT WOULD BE UNWISE TO DISPLEASE ME. THAT WAS HOW URI-TESHUP DIED.**

Ramesses looked at his large, timeworn hands. The world was placed into them. The future of the human race had been placed there. He was furious. The Hittites had been beaten at war! They were treating him as if he was a…buffer-zone prince! He spat. The idea made him sick.

Two powers ruled the ancient world. Anatolia was demanding that Egypt bow to her. This would never happen. The soul of the Pharaoh would never allow it to. So the answer translated to:

> **MURSILIS,**
> **WE ARE A PEACEFUL NATION. WE ARE NOT AFRAID OF ANATOLIA. IF YOU WILL HAVE WAR, HAVE WAR. WE ARE NOT AFRAID.**

He laughed. Mursilis would be vastly frustrated at this reply. He had to justify a declaration of war. He'd have to somehow claim that the Egyptians waged war first. Ramesses had given him nothing to take hold of. This was, truly, a good day's work.

~ ~ ~

Mursilis hit the wooden balcony post with his fist. It broke in two. Where was this war he wanted? Couldn't Ramesses give in or slip up? He sat back on his old throne and tried to think of a reply. Two seconds later a sword shot through the back of his throne and into his head. His thick skull shattered. His limp body remained upright because the sword held it so, staying in the back of the throne with a trickle of something grey.

Hantilis had killed the evil prince. Cloaked in white, he called the real Emperor over.

"Maybe you'll stop seeing him now!" Hattusillis laughed, pushing a weeping Padukhepa to the floor. "And yes, Nynetouckk…." Nynetouckk almost screamed. She was behind him. She didn't even know he knew her name. "I'll send the reply you want to Ramesses."

The reply which Hattusillis sent was read as this:

> **MY BROTHER RAMESSES,**
>
> **MURSILIS IS DEAD. I, HATTUSILLIS, THE RIGHTFUL EMPEROR, ADDRESS THIS DOCUMENT (TO YOU). I WILL IGNORE ANATOLIA AND DECLARE WAR UPON YOU INSTANTLY IF THE REPLY YOU SEND WASTES ANY MORE TIME.**

Rakesh told Istnofret in the unstable candlelight. Istnofret thanked her repeatedly for this. Ramesses really needed her. She couldn't sleep that night, her guilt-ridden head overwhelmed by love.

The process of sending emergency messages had indeed taken its time. A terrified Amon-Her-Khasimweh was able to reach Thebes one month after he set out.

The women weren't swooning over him now. Sand and wind wore lines into his skin. He had a straggly beard. He hadn't washed for a season. His eyebrows had become bushy and grey. He smelt like festering bird-grease. His white kilt had gone dark grey. It was more of a sandy, rock-torn rag than a piece of clothing. His hair was a palm tree. His strides were closer to those of a drunkard than a royal of the greatest civilisation on the planet. Blisters covered his feet and palms. Rough red patches highlighted rocky scratches on his knees. His arms were dressed in sores and sweat. His teeth had turned brown, his lips cut and swollen. The skin on his back was burnt and peeling. His face appeared to be covered in small red blotches. He coughed often; a desert-dry, insistent cough, which suggested that he might have caught a rare illness from other lands.

Those blue eyes were sore. Sand had rubbed them too much. His nose had become the colour of flames. His hair had grown to elbow length, matted by tough mud. He was filthy.

He staggered to the spot in the palace garden just behind the sacred pool. He saw a handsome young girl step outside the palace gates.

"I told her, Mbotus! And I never loved you!" she screamed. She leapt onto a camel and disappeared. Immediately, Amon-Her-Khasimweh knew.

The story—all of it—it all fell right into place. Why Rakesh came to Egypt in the first place. What Hattusillis had asked of her. Why she obeyed him. The part Mbotus played in all of this. Why the Hittite throne seemed so unstable. He knew it all. Adrenaline pumping through his body, he realised what the world stood to lose. He ran. He ran. He ran as if his soul was at stake.

Tionia sat in her warm Egyptian house with the warm Egyptian weather outside. Her hair had gone entirely grey. Her eyes still reflected lapping ocean waves. Her love was the bountiful ocean.

She didn't know of any of the state business going on. She slept soundly every night. Every night she dreamt the same, the dead Pharaoh reached out to her and asked; "Do you want to leave tonight? God will allow you to come to him when you are ready." Even this did not trouble her. For what it was worth, she dearly loved Akhenaten. He would be the way to the Aten, the Aten's dear son. She despaired that she couldn't chant his name for his continued existence without fear. His love ran towards her with open arms. In her faith she embraced it, and fell to her knees before its giver.

Pleasant thoughts drifted through her mind. How she needed to be set free! Still Akhenaten did not call her nearer. Something kept this fantastic lady on Earth.

She heard a loud knock at the door. She walked dreamily. Akhenaten had promised her immortality. She'd stop merely ambling through life after her death. Her Kha would float to the Aten. A smile seemed moulded upon the lady's face. She opened the door, her happiness radiating from her. Maybe, just maybe, there was enough space in the sky to hold everyone. Maybe Tutankhamun would be drinking wine with Amunhotep III and Akhenaten there.

Tionia didn't see the one she hoped for. There were two of them. One was the exhausted Prince Mbotus. His hair looked like a wet rat. His eyes shone with selfish tears. The other was a tired Pharaoh. His face was the image of anxiety. Tionia asked him what was happening. They pulled up stools to talk.

Ramesses explained the goings-on with the Hittites as quickly as he could. He told Tionia about the justified policy of keeping this secret from Istnofret. The mother nodded. From here on the Egyptian side, everything looked fair enough.

Prince Mbotus began to speak. He admitted his infatuation to Tionia. This made her smile. It was all too familiar to a sixty-year-old. He confessed as to how he had passed the events to Rakesh. This was due to a bad habit of giving the beauty everything she wanted. This gave her the power to fall on the Hittite side. Ramesses cut in, pointing out that Rakesh must have been communicating with someone, probably male, who held a constant support for Hattusillis.

They finished by saying that Ramesses had to speak with Istnofret in person. Only he could dull her fear and guilt. But where was she? Not in the palace. Not in the courtyard. They wondered. She might have revisited one of the temples. She might have been visiting her children, especially her baby Merneptah. They didn't know. They made the decision to stay in Tionia's house until Istnofret returned to it.

Someone shook the door at every knock. A man's voice was screaming that there was an emergency. Tionia was by now truly concerned. She opened the door to a greater-than-usual Amon-Her-Khasimweh.

"Brother!" shouted Ramesses, knocking the stool away as he stood up. The prince talked so quickly that what he said became incomprehensible. It ended with something about finding Istnofret.

Mbotus and Ramesses had no idea of her whereabouts. Prince Amon-Her-Khasimweh knew how serious this would be to her. He thought of what mattered most to her in the world. Only one name seemed to stand out. Rapidly, he thought back to the drunken discussions he'd had with Ramesses. He yelled something about a tree and ran outside. When the other three stepped out, they saw him running. They ran as fast as they could after him, but none could catch him.

Who could imagine the thoughts running through his head at that time? His mind seemed like his body. Somehow, he kept logic by his side.

Mbotus stayed back with Tionia. They couldn't run as fast as the rest. Ramesses had half flown from the palace to Tionia's house. He managed to run closest to Prince Amon-Her-Khasimweh of the three. Every other person felt worry for the prince. The public were alarmed.

The others had no idea of where Amon-Her-Khasimweh was taking them. It wasn't by the mud-brick houses. Those were long gone. It wasn't amongst the plaster-white houses.

They'd run in the other direction to those. The prince didn't slow down or glance around, so it wasn't the courtyard either...

Had she gone to the Nile? Despite the panic it glistened naturally. Sunlight fell like gold upon it. She could have gone there for the peace. Still Amon-Her-Khasimweh ran wildly. The doors of the Theban Court lay behind them. Mbotus became slower than Tionia, for he had run to find Ramesses, then to Tionia's house. He felt as if he was just about to collapse.

It was not just Amon-Her-Khasimweh who sensed the emergency. Tionia felt it too. Something somewhere had gone wrong.

The prince continued his tireless sprinting. His sore, blistered feet endured the fire-hot sand instinctively. He seemed to run with a limp. The journey back from northwest Africa had taken its toll. But he only had to run a little further...

The desert was a cat. It lay on its back and let its belly soak either the warmth or the rain. The cat played cruelly with sharp-edged stones there. It knocked them to one side or the other as it wished. This caused the prince great pain. His body needed more than anything then to rest and sleep. He forced it to suffer pain and endure a long run. This could only produce negative results.

Finally they arrived underneath the acacia, next to the Nile in the cooling shade.

Istnofret lay there with her chocolate eyes closed. Her skin looked young, tanned and beautiful. Her lips were red with cherry juice. That familiar blonde hair fell straight down to her chest. She wore her finest dress. Her perfume was expensive, her face a painted picture.

Her wrists crossed at her heart. The blood she had drawn from her wrists soaked her golden hair. It speckled starlets onto her elegant dress. Some ran into the life-giving Nile. If those lips could speak, they would utter one name. The Nile moved regardless.

An arrowhead dripping with blood lay nearby. For a moment, none present could speak. The sacrifice was incredible. Ramesses found himself wiping away a tear. Tionia knelt beside Istnofret to weep, Mbotus knelt beside her to comfort her.

By this time, Amon-Her-Khasimweh's face was soaked with tears. He ran over to the body of Istnofret. He kissed her for the first and last time. He took a bloody wrist and touched it as if it were a gem. He cradled her determined face and cried like he had never before. He supported her lifeless head and ran his fingers over her cold flesh. She wasn't returning for him.

Ramesses had been watching this passively. Shortly however, he raised his hand and told the prince; "Enough." He took the crying man away from her corpse and let him cry his tears upon strong shoulders.

Shaking with fear, Tionia digested the scene. Something had come back to her. As if in a trance, she got to her feet. Istnofret below her, she shuddered. She only whispered one thing. But she whispered it loud enough for everyone to hear.

"Love, my love," she repeated… I joined her as she bowed her head in respect.

Printed in the United Kingdom
by Lightning Source UK Ltd.
100747UKS00001B/35

9 781413 717488